MURDOCK

IRON HORSE LEGACY
BOOK EIGHT

ELLE JAMES

TWISTED PAGE INC

MURDOCK

IRON HORSE LEGACY BOOK #8

New York Times & *USA Today*
Bestselling Author

ELLE JAMES

© 2022 Twisted Page Inc. All rights reserved.

EBOOK ISBN: 978-1-62695-462-5

ISBN PRINT: 978-1-62695-461-8

Dedicated to my wonderful assistant Nora who keeps up with me and helps me in so many ways. She's also a great friend! That's the best part.

Elle James

AUTHOR'S NOTE

Enjoy other books in this series by Elle James

Visit ellejames.com for more titles and release
dates
Join her newsletter at
https://ellejames.com/contact/

CHAPTER 1

"THANK you for agreeing to meet with me at the ranch," Hank Patterson said as he cinched the girth and dropped the stirrup on the bay gelding he'd selected for Murdock to ride that afternoon.

"I put you off long enough," Sean Murdock said. "I figured I'd at least let you give your spiel before I told you I wasn't interested again."

Hank chuckled. "I appreciate your candor. If nothing else, I want to extend an open invitation to join the Brotherhood Protectors. You don't have to commit now. It could be when they finish the project at the Lucky Lady Lodge or a year or even two years down the road. I'm a patient man when it comes to hiring the best of the best."

"I don't know that I'd consider myself the best

of the best, but thanks for keeping the offer open. Right now, I'm happy to work in construction. For once, I'm not trying to kill anyone. It's satisfying seeing the fruits of my labors in demolished walls rather than the blood-soaked bodies of my enemies." His chest tightened as images of some of those enemies flitted through his mind.

"I get it," Hank said.

Murdock nodded. "I know you do. More than any of the civilians who've never served as a Navy SEAL, much less volunteered to serve their country in any branch of the military."

Hank stepped back from the horse and met Murdock's gaze. "Anyone who has served in combat finds it hard to assimilate into civilian life. Thankfully, being a part of the Brotherhood Protectors, we still rely on our training and skills. More importantly, we have the brotherhood of men who share similar experiences. Men who will have our backs. Brothers in arms. It doesn't get better than that." He tipped his head toward the gelding. "See if I lowered the stirrups enough."

Murdock's lips twisted. "It's been a long time since I've been on a horse. Even then, it was only for a couple of times."

Hank laughed. "It's like riding a bicycle that has

its own mind. Once you learn how you never forget."

"That's just it...I can count the number of times I've been on a horse on one hand. I don't consider that learning how. I prefer riding my bike." Murdock grabbed the horn, slipped his boot into the stirrup and swung his right leg over the saddle.

Hank handed him the reins. "Does that feel about right?"

Murdock nodded. "Seems like it."

"It's easy," Hank said as he mounted his dappled gray gelding like he'd been born to ride. Which he had, having grown up on the Iron Horse Ranch. "All you have to do is nudge him gently in the flanks with your heels to get him to go and pull back on the reins to stop. Little Joe is one of the gentlest horses on the ranch."

Murdock frowned as Little Joe danced sideways. "So you say."

"You'll be fine. Just follow me. We won't go out for long. I wanted to check on the vet who took one of the mares out half an hour earlier. They should've been back by now. Sadie wanted to make sure the vet stays for dinner. And dinner will be ready within an hour. I don't like to keep the others waiting."

Good. Murdock wasn't sure how long he'd last on the horse. The saddle was a lot harder than the seat of his motorcycle.

Hank led the way out of the barnyard into a wide pasture dotted with trees.

"Is it a requirement for your team to be able to ride a horse?"

Hank laughed. "Not at all. Up in the Crazy Mountains, you can get around on four-wheelers if you don't ride. Although, sometimes, a horse can get into places you can't go with a four-wheeler. And a horse doesn't run out of gas."

For the first hundred yards, Hank rode alongside Murdock, keeping the horses at a steady walk. Hank's gelding tossed his head and danced sideways several times.

Thankfully, Murdock's didn't seem to mind walking.

Hank glanced over at Murdock. "Ready to pick up the pace a little?"

Murdock snorted. "Whether I'm ready or not, your horse is ready."

With a twisted grin, Hank nodded. "He likes to run as soon as he leaves the barn. I'm trying to get him to cool his heels so that he doesn't think he can take off as soon as we leave the barnyard."

"Seems a shame to hold him back," Murdock said.

Hank nodded. "He loves to run."

Murdock shrugged. "In that case, let's go."

Hank frowned. "Just remember—"

"Pull on the reins to make him stop." Murdock held firmly to the reins. "Got it."

All Hank had to do was loosen his hold on the reins.

The horse leaped forward in a full gallop, kicking up a cloud of dust behind him.

Little Joe's ears perked, and his muscles bunched beneath the saddle.

"Oh, boy," Murdock murmured, his own body tensing. He much preferred his motorcycle to the unpredictability of a live animal.

Little Joe lunged forward.

Murdock slipped backward in the saddle, grabbed for the horn and held on for dear life as the gelding raced to catch up with Hank's horse.

Hank's mount topped a hill and disappeared down the other side.

Halfway up the hill, Little Joe ground to a halt and reared.

Still hanging onto the saddle horn, Murdock stayed on the upside of the horse. As Little Joe's front hooves hit the ground, he pitched forward and almost tipped over the horse's head.

The gelding made a quick turn to the left and ran with his ears pinned back.

Somewhere in the middle of trying to stay on the horse, Murdock lost the right rein. When he pulled back on the other, Little Joe turned left without slowing in the least.

"Whoa!" Murdock shouted.

The horse kept going as fast as he could, heading for a line of evergreen trees with low-lying branches. If he didn't stop the animal before the trees, Murdock would be scraped off by the first branch he encountered, possibly impaled or decapitated.

He pulled hard on the left rein. "Whoa!" he yelled.

Little Joe slowed a little, spun in a circle, came out of it and continued toward the trees.

Murdock's only other option was to bail, at the risk of breaking one—if not every—bone in his body. With little time to think, he slipped his boots to the very edge of the stirrups and braced his hands on the saddle horn.

As he lifted in the saddle, movement out of the corner of his left eye caught his attention.

A black horse raced toward him, its slim rider leaning over the animal's neck, cowboy hat riding low on his forehead. On a collision course with him, the two never slowed.

Murdock didn't have time to throw himself off Little Joe before the pair converged on them. At the last possible moment, the horse and rider turned sharply in the direction the bay gelding was heading and ran alongside them, quickly catching up.

The rider leaned dangerously sideways, the movement whipping the cowboy hat off his head, releasing a thick red ponytail from beneath.

Though concerned over staying alive, Murdock noted the rider wasn't a man at all but a female with long, fiery red hair.

She hooked her hand in the left rein and shouted, "Let go!"

Murdock released his hold on the rein and held onto the saddle.

The female wrapped the rein around her saddle horn, sat back in her saddle and pulled on her horse's reins.

Within less than two seconds, she brought the two horses to a halt just short of a giant pine.

Both horses shifted nervously, their sides heaving, coats slick with sweat.

"Are you all right?" the woman asked.

"I will be," he responded, uncurling his fingers from their death grip on the saddle, "as soon as I get off this horse."

"He's not going to run off with you as long as I have control over him," she said, reaching out to gather the other rein from beneath the horse's chin. She spoke to the horse in a calm, soothing tone. "It's okay. You're a good boy. Nothing's going to hurt you."

Murdock pulled his foot free of the left stirrup. "He might be a good boy for you, but I'd feel better with both feet on the ground."

The woman frowned. "It's a long walk back to the barn. Do you know how to get back?"

Murdock turned in the saddle, his brow dipping. "No idea."

She shook her head. "If you stay on the horse, I'll lead him back to the barn."

Murdock shook his head. "He might take off again." He lifted, ready to swing his left leg over.

"You should always mount and dismount from the left side of the horse. It confuses them if you get off on the right."

"I don't care if I slide off the back as long as I'm off this horse in the next two seconds." He sat back in the saddle.

The redhead shook her head and nudged her horse to one side, giving Murdock enough room to dismount on the left.

He quickly dropped to the ground and walked several steps away from the two horses and the one rider before he turned back, perturbed that he had no idea which direction to go. "Which way do I go?"

The redhead sighed. "It will take too long to get back if I walk my horse with you."

"Then point me in the right direction, and I'll get there on my own."

She shook her head. "I won't leave you out here to get lost again." She scooted forward, slipped her foot out of the left stirrup and tipped her head toward the back of the horse. "If you don't trust your horse, you can ride with me. Hop on."

Murdock held up his hands and backed away. "I'd rather not."

Her lips thinned. "And I'd like to get back to the barn before dark." She cocked a challenging red eyebrow. "Now, are you going to ride with me or ride your horse?"

9

He looked from Little Joe to the redhead and back to Little Joe.

The bay gelding turned his head, eyed Murdock and snorted.

Murdock could swear the animal was setting him up for another wild ride. "I don't think he likes me."

"He can sense your fear," the woman said. "Come on. Put your foot in my stirrup and swing up behind me."

"On the back of the horse? No saddle?" He shook his head. "No way."

"Fine." She slipped over the back of the saddle and settled on the horse's rump. "You can drive."

Murdock's eyes widened. "Nope." He shook his head. "I obviously don't know what I'm doing on a horse."

"A point we both can agree on." She climbed back into the saddle. "And we're wasting time. The sun is on its way down. Once it reaches the ridgeline, it'll be dark out here. I'm not equipped with a gun or a flashlight, and there are wolves and bears in these mountains. So, are you going to get on the back, or are we going to brave the wolves and bears?"

Murdock glanced around, his brow furrowing.

The sun was dangerously close to the ridgeline on its descent toward the horizon. He didn't know the way back, and he wouldn't put another person in danger of a wolf or bear attack because he was being a wuss about riding Little Joe.

Little Joe stomped his foot and snorted as if to say *make up your damned mind.*

"Until you and I come to an understanding, I'd rather ride with her," he told the horse.

The woman's lips twitched at the corners. She shifted forward in the saddle and left the stirrup empty for him.

"Grab the saddle horn and swing up like usual, only land behind the saddle." She leaned to her right, giving him the room he needed.

Murdock clutched the saddle horn, planted his boot in the stirrup and swung his leg over the back of the horse, landing hard on the animal's rump, not quite centered and off-balance.

The horse sidestepped toward Little Joe.

Little Joe snorted and pulled back, his movement arrested by the reins wrapped around the woman's saddle horn.

With both horses moving and himself barely balanced, Murdock wrapped his arms around the woman's waist and held on until he got his balance.

She pulled back on her horse's reins and spoke firmly, "Steady, girl."

The black mare calmed and stood still.

Murdock released his hold on the woman's slender waist and straightened.

"You'll want to hold onto me until we get back to the barn," she said. "It's okay. I don't bite…much."

"I can hold onto the saddle," he insisted, gripping the smooth leather.

"Have it your way," she said and gave her horse a healthy nudge.

The black mare lunged forward.

Murdock slid backward, his grip on the saddle doing little to keep him on the horse.

His rescuer pulled the horse to a stop.

"You made your point," he murmured and wrapped his arms around her waist.

She gave a curt nod and clicked her tongue.

The mare took off at a steady walk, heading back in the direction from which Murdock and Little Joe had come. At least, Murdock thought it was the right way.

"Is this your first time riding a horse?" the woman asked.

"No," he admitted. "But this is my first time riding in a decade and the first time on a runaway."

"Most people never forget how to ride, even after a decade."

"My riding experience consists of three times on a 25-year-old hack at a rent-a-horse riding stable when I was a teen. I don't think it counts," he said.

"Ah," she said. "That explains it."

He hated that she was so smug about his lack of riding skills, but he couldn't argue with her. He had no horse skills to brag about, and she did.

"Considering I'm closer to you than I'd be with a stranger at a Rave concert, it would be nice to know who you are," he said, his mouth next to her ear, her curly red hair tickling his nose.

She laughed. "I can't picture you at a rave, much less a rock concert."

He shrugged. "Granted, I've never been to a rave, but I have been to a rock concert."

"When?" she demanded. "About the time you last rode a horse?"

"Busted." His heart warmed at the humor in her

tone. "I was a teen when I went to my last rock concert in San Diego."

"San Diego?" she half-turned, her face so close to his he could have easily tasted her lips. His heart skipped several beats before it thundered against his ribs. "You grew up in San Diego?"

"I did," he said.

"I should've guessed you hadn't grown up here in Montana," she said.

He chuckled. "What was your first clue?"

"Many, if not all, young men who grew up in Montana have an understanding of horses."

"And I don't," he concluded.

She nodded. "I know Little Joe. If he was running away, he was spooked by something. All it would take to slow him down was a firm hand and some sweet talk."

"Being as I don't know Little Joe and what works to get through to him, I was just along for one helluva ride." His arms tightened slightly around her waist as he recalled the harrowing race across the hard-packed earth, aiming for a painful collision with a stand of trees.

"I can't believe you were out here riding on your own," she said.

"I wasn't. I was following Hank Patterson when Little Joe took a detour."

She nodded. "Hank will be looking for you."

"Or what's left of me after his horse took me on a one-way trip to hell," Murdock commented.

"If he doesn't find you soon, he'll head back to the barn. Most horses head back to the barn when they lose their rider."

Murdock's lip curled. "Nice to know they don't feel the least bit responsible or protective."

"They just know where they'll get their next meal," the redhead said.

"You know a lot about the ranch," Murdock said.

"I should," she said, her tone flat. "Besides the fact that I'm a large animal veterinarian, I've known Hank Patterson most of my life. We live in a small community."

Murdock sighed. "Then I'm sure you and Hank will get a laugh out of rescuing me from a runaway horse that is the tamest on the Iron Horse Ranch."

"I doubt that seriously. Hank is a good guy. If you came out here with Hank, he'll be worried about you. The sooner we get you back to the barn, the better. And if Hank isn't back, I'll find him and let him know Little Joe is all right."

It figured she'd mention the horse was safe, not necessarily Murdock. He could tell where the woman's loyalties lay. It made sense since she was a veterinarian.

"Gabbie Myers," she said.

"Gabbie Myers?" he asked.

"My name," she said. "I'm Gabbie Myers. And you are?"

"Sean Murdock," he said. "Most people just call me Murdock."

"Murdock," she repeated. "Sounds important. How do you know Hank?"

"We're both Navy SEALs," Murdock said.

Again, Gabbie turned her head, her eyebrow raised. "I knew Hank was a SEAL, but *you* were, too?"

He frowned. "I might not know my way around horses," he said, "however, I lived through BUD/S training and thirteen deployments."

She patted his hand resting on her midsection. "Sorry. I didn't mean that to sound derogatory. It's just that I know Hank. I don't believe there's a thing he can't do. I guess I expected all Navy SEALs to be the same."

"Ouch. That hit below the belt," he said, tamping down a flush of anger at being judged and coming up short of this woman's expectations. Not that it mattered. She meant nothing to him. Although he did find her strangely attractive in an athletic, kick-ass way. What woman had he known who could stop a runaway horse without falling out of her saddle? Still, he felt the need to explain his horseback-riding shortcomings. "I didn't grow up on a ranch like Hank. I grew up in San Diego. If anything, I'm more accustomed to water than a saddle."

"I guess, since you were in the Navy, that makes sense." Gabbie shot a glance over her shoulder. "Please, don't be offended by my comment. Hank is the only Navy SEAL I know. Though, I understand he's hired others over the past few years since he returned to Montana. I've been too busy to get to know them personally."

His mild anger subsiding, he loosened his hold around her middle. Her horse had settled into a rhythmic gait.

"Think you can keep from falling off if we speed things up a bit?" she asked. "I was supposed to be back at the barn a while ago. I'm sure Hank will be gathering a search party for the both of us. I don't want them gone on their search when we arrive back at the barn."

"Do what you have to," he said. "I'll do my best not to further disgrace myself in your eyes."

"Wow, that makes me sound heartless." Gabbie shook her head. "I didn't mean to insult you." She sighed. "I'm not always good with my social skills, much preferring the company of animals to humans. That said, I promise not to trot too much and jar your insides."

"Thanks." Murdock braced himself, tightened his arms around her waist and held on.

The redhead nudged her horse with her heels and clicked her tongue.

The black mare increased her speed to a trot.

The motion bounced Murdock, jolting his teeth together until the horse transitioned from the trot into a smooth gallop.

Immediately, the jolting motion ended, replaced by a rocking motion Murdock could live with. He held on around Gabbie's waist, determined to stay upright for the duration of the ride back to the barn. With his body pressed against hers, he matched her rhythm and the sway of her body. The woman rode as if one with the horse.

The sun had dipped below the ridge, the sunshine fading quickly into darkness. Not long afterward, lights appeared ahead, shining from the windows of the ranch house and the exterior flood light in front of the barn.

A group of men mounted on horseback passed through the gate into the pasture.

Gabbie shook her head. "Trust Hank to rustle up a posse at the drop of a hat."

A shout went up. The man pulled their horses to a halt and waited for Gabbie and Murdock's arrival.

As they neared the posse, Gabbie slowed her horse to a trot and then a walk, coming to a halt in front of the man on the lead horse. "Hank." She tipped her head toward the man behind her. "I found this guy on a runaway horse. Does he belong to you? Or should I shoot him for trespassing?"

Hank laughed along with the other men gathered around. "Save your bullet. He's with us." His gaze met Murdock's. "Sorry. By the time I realized you weren't right behind me, you were long gone. I thought for sure Little Joe had gotten the bit between his teeth and headed for the barn. When I got back to the barn, and you weren't there, I gathered the team I had available. We were on our way out to find you." He smiled at Gabbie. "I see you found our local vet."

Murdock's lips twisted. "She found me and rescued me from being scraped out of my saddle in a stand of trees."

Hank shook his head. "Something must've spooked Little Joe. He's usually the most laid-back horse in my herd."

Murdock let go of his hold on Gabbie's waist and slid off the back of the horse, backing away as soon as his feet hit the ground.

Hank grinned. "I take it your first time back in the saddle wasn't encouraging."

Murdock shook his head. "If it weren't for Dr. Myers, I'd be a carcass for the wolves and bears to scavenge."

"We'd have found you before it came to that," Hank said. "Are you okay? Nothing broken or hurt?"

Murdock's lips twisted, "Nothing but my pride."

He turned and gave Gabbie a slight bow. "Thank you, Miss Myers, or should I call you Dr. Myers?"

Gabbie's cheeks turned a soft shade of pink in the light shining down from the barn. "Gabbie's fine. I'm not much on formality."

"Don't let her fool you," Hank said with a smile.

"She worked hard for that title, graduating top of her class in vet school. We're damned glad she chose to practice close to home. The only other large animal vet in the county wants to retire at the end of the year. We need her."

"You knew I'd come home," Gabbie said.

"We hoped you would," Hank said, his voice softening. "And we're glad you did." He glanced around at the men with him. "Guys, this is Sean Murdock, Navy SEAL."

"Fresh meat for the team?" a tall man with white-blond hair and broad shoulders said with a grin."

Hank shook his head. "Murdock is working at the Lucky Lady Lodge in the McKinnon's efforts to renovate the lodge since the explosion in the mine damaged some of the structure." His gaze met and held Murdock's. "I'm hoping that he'll come to work with us when the construction is done."

The big guy with the light blond hair dropped down from his saddle and held out his hand. "I've seen your dossier. I'm Axel Svenson. Most folks call me Swede."

When Murdock gripped the man's hand, he stared into ice-blue eyes. "Navy SEAL, right?"

Swede nodded. "Guilty."

Murdock had heard of Swede from members of his former SEAL team. The man had a reputation that lived on in tales of prior battles, capturing Taliban leaders and more. "I've heard of you."

"All good, I hope." Swede released Murdock's hand and shoved his through his short-cropped hair, making it stand on end.

Murdock grinned. "Legendary."

Swede chuckled. "Hear that, Hank? Legendary." His chest puffed out. "I like the sound of that. Do you think Allie will agree?"

"My sister thinks the sun rises and sets on you," Hank said. "But legendary?" He shook his head. "She'd want to make sure your head didn't swell."

Swede's lips pressed together. "Way to poke a hole in a man's ego."

Hank, along with the other man and woman with him, laughed. "You'll get over it." Hank slid out of his saddle.

The others followed suit.

Murdock reached up to help Gabbie down.

She frowned and shook her head.

"Right," Murdock said. "This isn't your first rodeo." He stepped back and let her get down on her own, which she did with a fluid grace only years of riding could produce.

Hank turned to the man with salt and pepper gray hair and a woman with a short cap of auburn curls. "This is Vince Van Cleave and his wife, Dallas Hayes. Both former Army. Both part of the Brotherhood Protectors team."

The female gripped his hand and gave it a firm shake. "I've heard a lot about you. You'd make a great addition to the team."

"Thank you. But I traded in my rifle for a hammer," Murdock said. "It's nice to shoot nails and build something rather than shooting bullets and killing people."

"That's a shame," the man beside her said and shook Murdock's hand. "I hear you were a sniper and skilled at hand-to-hand combat."

Murdock dipped his head in acknowledgment. "Not much use for those skills here. But I am getting good at knocking out walls and breaking up tiles. And I'm a helluva a good shot with a nail gun. I'll stick to that for now. Vince? Is that right?"

The man laughed. "Yeah, but I don't go by that name. Most of the guys call me Viper."

"Viper." Murdock tipped his chin. "Got it."

"Nice to meet you," Viper said.

"Same." And Murdock meant it. The Special Operations community was tight-knit and looked out for each other. Already, he felt comfortable around the men and women Hank had brought together. But he wasn't in the market to be a mercenary. He wanted nothing to do with combat, protective services or high-intensity work. Tearing out walls and rebuilding them was what he wanted to do.

A bell rang from the back porch of the house.

Hank shot a glance in that direction. "We'd better get the horses put up, clean up and get to the dinner table. Sadie prepared pot roast, potatoes and corn on the cob, and I'm starving."

Murdock rounded Little Joe, giving him a wide berth in case the beast decided to plant a hoof in his face.

Gabbie leaned close and whispered in his ear, "When going around the back of a horse. It's always good to lay your hand on the horse to let it know that you're there and in which direction you're going. That way, you don't spook them, and they also can't get enough power behind a leg to cause you too much damage."

Not liking that feeling of complete inadequacy

he'd gotten on his short ride with Little Joe, Murdock listened to Gabbie's advice.

"Thanks," he said. "And just so you know, if I stay in this area, I *will* learn to ride."

She gave him a wide grin. "I hope you do." Gabbie led her horse and Little Joe into the barn, the smile still curling her lips.

Murdock stood for a moment, wondering what she'd meant by her last comment. Did she only hope he'd learn to ride? Or did she hope he'd stay in the area?

Curious now, he followed her into the barn, wanting to know more about this woman who was a licensed veterinarian and an accomplished rider. Even more than that, her strength and fearlessness were sexy as hell. He had to know more.

CHAPTER 2

GABBIE SHOWED MURDOCK, by example, how to care for his horse. She removed her mount's saddle and saddle blanket, stored them in the tack room then quickly and efficiently brushed her and led her to a stall where she fed the animal two sections of hay and a bucket of grain.

Murdock watched her closely when he could have watched any of the other men.

His gaze on her didn't make her uncomfortable, but it did make her more aware of him and the way he moved like the man with a military background that he was...shoulders back, confident and sure of himself, even though he wasn't sure of his horse.

When he'd ridden behind her, holding her

around her waist, she'd been hyper-aware of his muscular arms and the solid chest pressed against her back. But it was his thighs pressed against hers that had made her blood burn through her veins like molten lava.

Gabbie might be skilled with animals and knew most of the long-standing residents of Eagle Rock and the surrounding ranches, but she had little experience with intimate relationships.

For so many years, her focus had been on her studies and making the best grades she could. Her grades had earned her scholarships to continue her education toward her ultimate goal of attaining her Doctorate in Veterinary Medicine.

She was no virgin, but the sex she'd had during her undergraduate degree schooling had been awkward and dissatisfying. It made her wonder what all the hype was about desire and orgasms. Was it her, or had she chosen the wrong partner? She'd suspected it was her.

Hank, Swede, Viper and Dallas quickly dealt with their horses, turning them loose in the pasture behind the barn.

"You can release Little Joe with the others," Hank said. "Gabbie's mare will stay the night in the barn. I'll let her out in the morning." He paused beside Gabbie. "You're staying for dinner, aren't you?"

Gabbie frowned. "I should get back to the clinic. I have to leave out early tomorrow morning for a delivery."

"You have to eat sometime. You might as well eat with us. Besides, Sadie will be disappointed if you don't stay. She wanted to thank you for all you've done for her mare."

Gabbie shook her head, a smile twitching the corners of her lips. "Why is a megastar like Sadie McClain preparing dinner for me? She should have a personal chef or something."

Hank frowned. "She only has the chef when she's at her house in Los Angeles and working on a movie. Here on the ranch, she likes to cook. And she's really good. You would know that if you stayed for dinner." He winked. "So, what's it to be? Go home to eat leftovers or nothing at all? Or stay and make my wife happy because she gets to show off her cooking skills?"

Gabbie laughed. "When you put it like that, I'd be ungrateful to leave without sharing a meal with you and Sadie." She sighed. "I'll stay. But I need to leave soon after."

"Deal." Hank nodded toward the barn door. "Ready to head up to the house?"

She shook her head. "I want to check on the mare one more time before I come up. You can go on without me." She nodded toward Murdock. "I'll bring your recruit up with me when he's done with Little Joe."

Hank nodded. "Thanks for helping out today. I wouldn't have put him on any other horse. Little Joe is as solid as they come."

"Something spooked him. It could've happened to any horse."

Hank's lips twisted. "Unfortunately, it happened to a green rider."

She patted his arm. "Don't worry. He's already said he wants to learn to ride."

Hank sighed. "Good. It helps to know how to ride in these parts. Especially if he comes to work with us."

"What exactly does your team do?" Gabbie asked.

"Whatever it takes to protect people, a place or extract someone from a bad situation the police, military or anyone else can't touch."

Her eyes widened. "Is there a big demand for such protective services?"

He nodded. "More than you'd think."

Gabbie frowned. "I might want to hire you for my trip tomorrow."

"Seriously? Are you worried about your delivery?"

She tipped her head toward the door. "Go to the house. We can talk about it over dinner."

"I'll hold you to that," Hank said. "See you in a few minutes."

"We'll be right behind you," Gabbie promised.

Murdock had just finished brushing Little Joe when Gabbie approached him. "Is he ready to go out to the pasture?"

"I don't know the routine. Am I supposed to give him hay and grain like you did for the mare?" Murdock asked.

Gabbie shook her head. "No. Just release him in the pasture. He'll graze. I'm keeping the mare for another night in a stall. She recently recovered from colic. We wanted her to have another day of grain before she's released to the pasture." She loosened the straps of the bridle, slipped it over the gelding's head and snapped a lead onto his halter. Rather than walk him out herself, she handed the lead to Murdock and walked with him and Little Joe out to the pasture gate.

She opened the gate.

He led the horse through it.

"Unclip the lead," she said. "Little Joe knows what to do from there."

Murdock released the gelding.

Instead of running off as most horses did once released, Little Joe stood beside Murdock and nudged his arm with his nose.

"Now, you're playing nice?" Murdock laughed and rubbed the horse's nose. "What had you spooked, big guy?"

The horse tossed his head and nickered softly.

Murdock reached up and scratched behind the animal's ears. When he stopped scratching, the horse nudged him again.

"You're like an overgrown puppy." Murdock rubbed the horse's nose and smiled at Gabbie.

Standing in the starlight, his teeth glowing a bluish-white, he made Gabbie's heart beat faster and butterflies erupt in her belly. "Little Joe is a fairly docile animal. He had to have been frightened by something to react the way he did."

"I thought I saw something slither in front of us before he reared and bolted."

Gabbie nodded. "We have a healthy population

of snakes in the Crazy Mountains, including the rattlesnake."

Little Joe nuzzled Murdock's shoulder again.

"Sorry. I have to go. Maybe the next time I come, I'll bring an apple or a carrot." He smoothed his hand over the horse's neck and stepped through the gate, closing it behind him. He smiled at Gabbie and held out his arm. "Can I escort you to the ranch house? I have a long way to go to redeem myself after losing my pride so completely on Little Joe."

Gabbie's cheeks heated as she hooked her hand through the crook of his arm. "You don't have a reason to redeem yourself. You stayed on the horse. Most people would've lost their seat when he reared." She looked up at him. "Actually, I'm impressed you were still in the saddle."

He chuckled. "I was just about to jump when you showed up to rescue me. I owe you."

She shook her head. "No, you don't. Anyone would've done what I did."

He snorted. "Not everyone is as skilled a rider. You were amazing."

Her chest swelled, and her heart beat faster. It was too bad they'd part ways after dinner. She might never see him again. Then again, it was a small town. "Hank said you're working at the Lucky Lady Lodge."

He nodded as they climbed the stairs to the back porch that stretched the length of the rambling ranch house Hank and Sadie had built when the old house had burned to the ground.

"I'm working with a group of former Special Operations guys. We've all traded our guns for hammers and are all in on the remodel of the lodge."

"Any idea how long you'll be working there?" she asked, trying not to sound too interested. Her breath caught and held as she waited for his response.

"As far as I can tell, as long as it takes. Molly McKinnon and her fiancé, Parker Bailey, want to restore the old place to its former glory and upgrade the amenities in the process. They're aiming for Christmas to complete the renovations."

"Five more months. That's ambitious," Gabbie said. "The old lodge took a hit with the explosions in the mine."

"We were briefed on the trouble they had." He frowned as he held the door for her to enter the house. "Mollie's dad is lucky to be alive."

"Yes, he is." Gabbie's lips pressed together. "I remember the dozens of men combing the hills for the missing McKinnon patriarch. We all thought he was dead." She smiled tightly. "Thankfully, the McKinnon siblings never gave up."

"They're an amazing family from what I've seen so far. I'm glad to be a part of their vision to rebuild such a historic landmark."

"How's that going?" she asked as she led him down the hallway to the bathroom where they could wash up. The door was open. She waved toward the sink. "You can go first."

"No reason we can't both wash our hands at the same time." He waited for her to enter and followed her inside.

Gabbie squirted soap into her hands and turned on the faucet.

While she washed her hands, he answered her question. "We're done with the demolition side of the renovation and have started rebuilding the damaged walls and supports. It's coming along."

She shook the water from her hands and reached for the hand towel. "I'm surprised you're here on a weekday."

He soaped his hands and rinsed them beneath the running water. "We're at a standstill, waiting for lumber. Supplies have been hard to come by in the past few weeks. That's why I'm here today instead of working at the lodge. Hank found out we were at loose ends and asked me to come out to the ranch. Molly said I might as well."

When Gabbie handed him the towel, their fingers brushed against each other. A shock of electricity ripped through her system, making her pulse quicken and her breath catch in her throat. She stood still, unable to move, to speak, the force of awareness so strong, it left her unable to think straight.

What was wrong with her? She had always led a focused life, completely committed to her studies and then her job. One chance rescue, and she was acting like a teenager crushing on the star quarterback who was completely out of her league.

This man had been all over the world, met hundreds of people and probably had any girl he wanted.

Gabbie had barely been out of Montana. What interest would he have in someone like her...a geek and socially inept woman, cursed with fiery red hair and freckles. She wasn't even pretty.

She released her breath with a sigh.

His brow wrinkled. "Why the long face and sigh?"

Her cheeks heated. Was she that easy to read? "No reason. I'm just tired, and I have a long day tomorrow."

"You were telling Hank something about delivering a horse?" Murdock stepped out into the hallway.

Gabbie followed. "Yeah. I—"

"There you are," Hank called out from the end of the hall. "We're waiting on you in the dining room."

Gabbie grimaced. "Guess we'd better get a move on before they all get hangry."

She led the way to the dining room, where Hank stood at the head of the table with Sadie McClain at his side.

Everyone waited until Gabbie and Murdock entered the room before they claimed their seats.

Hank waved a hand toward the two empty seats near Sadie. "We saved you two places."

Murdock held Gabbie's chair as she took her seat, then he settled beside her, his shoulder brushing hers.

Another rush of heat raced through her.

She sat still for a moment, willing her breathing to return to normal and her mind to engage.

Sadie sat beside Gabbie and reached out to squeeze her hand. "Thank you for taking care of Licorice. She seemed so much better when I rode her yesterday."

Gabbie sucked in a breath and focused on Sadie, not the man on her other side, stirring her insides into a frenzy. "She's back to a hundred percent. No signs of colic, and she was full of energy on our ride."

Murdock leaned close to Gabbie. "Is Licorice the black mare we rode back to the barn?"

She nodded and smiled at Sadie. "She felt good enough to chase down Little Joe, who'd spooked and taken off with Murdock. I'd say she's back in top form."

"I'm so relieved," Sadie said.

"You caught it early enough that treatment was swift and effective," Gabbie assured the beautiful blond actress who'd grown up on the ranch where Hank had ultimately set up his Brotherhood Protectors organization. She could have lived anywhere else in the world, but she'd chosen to come home.

Gabbie understood why. She didn't have to set

up her veterinary practice in Eagle Rock, but she couldn't think of anywhere else she'd rather be. She loved the town, the people and the Crazy Mountains.

Platters of food made their way around the table as each person loaded their plate with the juicy roast, garlic-roasted potatoes, corn on the cob and salad.

"Where are the babies?" Gabbie asked Sadie.

Sadie smiled. "I fed them just a little while ago and settled them down for the night. They had a busy day. Chuck Johnson and his wife Kate brought Lyla over to play with Emma. Little McLain crawled all over the place, trying to keep up with them. By the time Chuck's family left, Emma and McClain were exhausted. They're sound asleep." Sadie's face shone with her love for her children, making Gabbie just a little envious of her. Not for her mega-stardom but for her happy life as Hank's wife and the mother of two beautiful, healthy children.

Now that Gabbie had her license and was fully engaged as a practicing veterinarian, she had time to think about her next goal in life. Should she specialize in her practice? Or could she finally find time to have a life. Maybe even one like Sadie and Hank's or Chuck and Kate's.

As an only child, Gabbie had always wanted a brother or sister. When that hadn't happened, and her mother and father had retired to Florida, she'd thought about having children of her own. Trouble was, she hadn't found the time in her busy schedule to date. Hell, she hadn't found anyone even mildly interesting enough to strike up a conversation with.

The thigh brushing against hers sent a ripple of excitement racing along her nerve endings.

A little voice in her mind whispered, *What about Murdock?*

"Gabbie, you said you have to pick up a horse tomorrow?" Hank said, his eyebrows raised. "What's that about?"

She nodded, pulling her thoughts away from the man beside her. "Yes. I'm supposed to be at the Double Diamond Ranch to pick up a horse at five-thirty in the morning."

"Is the horse sick?" Sadie asked.

Gabbie shook her head. "No. Just the opposite. He's in perfect health and going to his new owner at a ranch west of Anaconda, outside a little town called Last Resort."

Hank frowned. "Last Resort... Wasn't that town in the news recently?"

Swede lowered his fork. "As I recall, a man was arrested for shooting at cars passing on the road going through the area."

Hank nodded. "That's right. He said they were trespassing and that Last Resort had seceded from the United States and was a separate country in its own right." He frowned across the table at Gabbie. "The ranch is on the other side of Last Resort?"

She nodded. "And you just outlined my concern."

"Can you bypass Last Resort by coming from another direction?" Hank asked.

"I looked at the map. Coming in from the opposite direction would add three hours to my two-hour trip. There's a mountain range I'd have to go around to approach from the west."

Swede had his cell phone out with the map pulled up. "She's right. Still, it might be worth the additional three hours to avoid Last Resort. From what I read, the town is full of hard right preppers, who are all prepared for doomsday to the point they've been accused of plotting doomsday."

"Oh, sweetie," Sadie laid her hand on Gabbie's arm, "you can't go through there. That's too dangerous. If you really have to go, you need to take the extra time to go the long way."

Gabbie shook her head. "The guy who bought the horse is paying me enough for the transport that I can afford to purchase and install a large x-ray machine in my clinic. I can't pass up this opportunity. Besides, they arrested the man who was shooting at passersby. It should be safe to go through there now."

Swede looked up from his phone and shook his head. "He's out on bail."

Gabbie sighed. "Then I'll just have to take the long way around."

"How close is the ranch to Last Resort?" Swede asked.

"Five miles to the west," Gabbie answered. "That's what's so frustrating."

Murdock frowned. "What if the buyer is one of the preppers espousing Last Resort and the surrounding area as a sovereign nation?"

Gabbie's brow dipped. "I hadn't thought of that. His name is Michael Howard."

Hank shook his head. "Doesn't ring a bell."

Swede was busy typing with his thumbs on his cell phone. "Michael Howard isn't coming up with anything significant. I did find a former financial advisor, Michael Howe, involved in a Ponzi scheme. He was accused of bilking investors out of millions but was acquitted when the head of the firm, Jack Paulson, pleaded guilty and took the blame. Paulson spent one month in federal prison before he was found unresponsive in his prison bed with a plastic bag cinched tightly over his head." Swede looked up. "It's been five years, and they never determined who killed him."

"Not the kind of people you want to get sideways with," Viper commented.

Dallas leaned into Viper. "Not anyone I'd want to have dealings with."

Gabbie's gut clenched. "Wow. If my client's name was Michael Howe, I'd back out of the transfer, but his name is Howard, not Howe. And I've already paid the medical supply company for the x-ray machine." She squared her shoulders. "Besides, that was five years ago. The Michael Howard I'm going to meet isn't the Michael Howe who worked with Paulson."

Sadie squeezed her hand. "Honey, why take the chance? Passing through Last Resort is bad enough."

"I'm only going to deliver a horse," Gabbie

insisted. "As far as I know, he's just a man who bought a horse."

"A very expensive horse," Murdock said, "that he might be paying for with money he stole from duped investors."

"It's all conjecture," Gabbie said. "And I don't want to take the horse on a five-hour trip when I can make the same trip in two hours."

Sadie patted her hand. "If you're sure you want to go, then at least let Hank send one of his protectors along with you."

Gabbie met Hank's gaze. "You'd do that for me?"

"Absolutely," Hank said.

Viper held up a hand. "Dallas or I would go, but we're scheduled to meet with a client tomorrow morning."

"We could call and reschedule," Dallas offered.

"That's not necessary," Hank said. "Everyone else is on assignment, but I can go with Gabbie."

"I can reschedule my visit to the hospital in Bozeman," Sadie said.

Hank frowned. "That's right. I had daddy duty tomorrow."

Sadie nodded. "But I'm sure I can reschedule and stay home with Emma and McClain."

"The patients will be disappointed," Hank said.

"It'll be okay," Sadie said. "Gabbi needs you to go with her."

"I'll go," Murdock said.

Gabbie turned to the man beside her. "But you don't work for Hank."

"Does it matter?" Murdock asked. "We're on hold at the lodge until more supplies arrive. Molly and Parker won't mind if I take another day off."

Hank grinned. "It's one of the many kinds of service we offer our clients. You could consider this a trial run for working as a Brotherhood Protector."

"I'd do it whether or not I worked for Brotherhood Protectors," Murdock said. "I owe her for rescuing me."

Gabbie shook her head. "You don't owe me anything."

"Fine," he said. "I'm still going with you." He glanced across at Hank. "If that's okay with you."

Hank nodded. "It's perfect. And, before you leave the house, let me equip you with whatever you might need should you run into any trouble."

"I have my own handgun," Murdock said.

"Good," Hank nodded at the table. "Let's finish eating this wonderful food our chef has provided;

then we can talk shop in the Brotherhood Protectors' headquarters."

The rest of the meal was spent in relative silence, everyone concentrating on finishing the food on their plate.

Finally, Sadie laughed and tossed her napkin on the plate. "I'm done if you're waiting on me to finish."

"Are you sure?" Hank asked. "The roast was perfect, and the potatoes... Everything was great."

"Yes, the food was great," Murdock said, his words echoing around the table.

"Thank you," Sadie said. "Leave the dishes on the table. I'm going down with you."

As one, they rose from the table and followed Hank to a door on the far side of the massive living room. He leaned close to a retinal scanner. A light flashed, and the door opened to a staircase leading down into a darkened basement.

As soon as Hank set foot on the top step, the staircase lit up. He descended quickly.

Gabbie followed with Murdock close behind her.

At the bottom of the staircase, an enormous room spread out before them with a large conference table and a display screen at one end. In a far corner of the room was an array of monitors and a row of computer keyboards.

Swede took a seat in front of the monitors, his hands flying over the keyboard.

Hank waved toward a room to his right. "Let me show you what we have available to our team, depending on the mission." When he opened the door, the interior light automatically blinked on.

Gabbie gasped.

Inside were racks of every type of weapon imaginable, including some that might not be legal to own as a civilian.

"You should be all right with your own handgun, but you might want to take a high-powered rifle, just in case." Hank nodded toward what appeared to be military-grade semi-automatic rifles. "Then again, you might not want to be that obvious, going into prepper territory. They might see you as a threat."

"I'll stick with my Glock," Murdock said.

Hank nodded and moved to a set of shelves and drawers against one wall. "Definitely take some communications equipment. If you two get separated, at least you can stay in contact." Hank pulled a small duffle bag off a shelf and loaded what appeared to be earbuds, walkie-talkies and night vision goggles inside.

He reached into a small drawer and pulled out a necklace with a shiny pendant dangling from the chain. "Gabbie, you need to wear this at all times. If you get lost or separated from Murdock, he can track you with this." He flashed a hand-held device in front of her and tucked it into the bag. "We can also track you on our computer here."

Murdock took the necklace from Hank's hand and stepped behind Gabbie.

She lifted her ponytail out of the way, allowing him to secure the necklace around her neck. When his fingers brushed against her skin, she shivered deliciously.

Murdock rested his hands on her shoulders. "Don't lose that."

She nodded, her heart pounding against her ribs.

Viper held up a block of what looked like clay and some metal pieces. "You shouldn't go anywhere without a little C-4 in case you need to get someone's attention or need to blow a door." He added the plastic explosives to the bag.

"I'm delivering a horse," Gabbie protested, "not going to war."

"It's better to have too much than not enough," Hank said. "Are you sure you don't need a rifle?"

"On second thought, yes," Murdock said.

Hank handed him one of the rifles that looked like what the military carried. "It's basically the same model as the M4A1 you carried on active duty, tricked out with many of the same features as the SOFMOD upgrade."

Gabbie touched the metal pendant, her head spinning with all Hank had stored in the basement of his home. "Is this all necessary?"

Murdock stepped in front of her and took her hands in his. "Probably not. The thing is, we don't know what to expect. And we're always better safe than sorry."

He met and held her gaze with his incredibly blue eyes. "Do you trust me?"

She frowned. "I just met you." Her frown eased, and she gave him a crooked smile. "But yes. For some strange reason, I do."

CHAPTER 3

AFTER THEIR EVENTFUL DAY, Murdock stashed the duffle bag in Gabbie's truck and followed her to Eagle Rock on his motorcycle. She parked at her clinic, which was a large metal barn with living quarters in what had once been the loft. He'd left her there and gone to the Lucky Lady Lodge, where he met with Molly and PJ, who'd stayed late to man the bar when the bartender called in sick.

Molly and Parker had insisted he go with Gabbie, as concerned for her safety as Hank and Sadie had been.

Murdock had a beer with the other members of his construction team and explained where he'd be the following day. Each man had been a member of special operations units on active duty.

He'd served with Drake Morgan in the Navy SEALs and worked with Grimm, Michael Reaper, and Judge, Joe Smith, when the Delta Force Operators had teamed with the SEALs on a joint operation to take out Taliban terrorists. Pierce Turner, or Utah, was former Marine Force Reconnaissance, and they'd worked to extract a Marine platoon pinned down by the Taliban.

All skilled fighters, now semi-skilled carpenters, they'd all vowed to avoid conflict, but so far, they hadn't been completely successful.

"We all signed on to rebuild this lodge, but it seems we're destined to do so much more," Drake said.

"Can't seem to get away from the fight, can we?" Grimm agreed.

"Hopefully, there will be no fight, and I'll be back to work the day after tomorrow," Murdock said.

Grimm snorted. "You just jinxed yourself."

"Maybe we should come along as your backup," Utah said.

"I really don't think we'll need it," Murdock insisted. "We're just going to drop off a horse and come right back."

Judge stared across the table at Murdock. "What's your gut telling you?"

Murdock paused with his longneck beer bottle poised halfway to his mouth. He glanced across at Drake. "Remember when we went into that Afghan village that was supposed to be only civilians?"

Drake nodded. "Before we went in, you told me it didn't feel right."

"And it wasn't. It was a trap full of Taliban waiting to wipe out our team." Murdock's lips pressed into a tight line. "I have the same feeling now."

Drake's brow furrowed. "Then, we definitely need to go with you."

Murdock shook his head. "If my gut is wrong, going in heavily manned and armed will only stir up the preppers. Gabbie and I should be able to get in and out without getting anyone up in arms." His gaze slipped around to each of his team members. "But be ready in case I need you. And Hank will also have my back. He has resources I've only just begun to realize."

Drake nodded. "He's got a network of people across the country. If you get in a tight spot, he'll help."

"And so will we," Utah reiterated.

They all agreed.

Murdock left his beer half full and went to his room, determined to get a couple of hours of sleep. He showered and laid out his clothes, boots, Glock and extra magazines full of bullets. If all went well, he wouldn't have to use them.

If not, he would be prepared.

When he lay down on top of the comforter, he stared up at the ceiling and thought back over the day, the runaway horse and the fierce redhead who'd swooped in to save him. He only hoped he'd be as successful protecting her as she had been with him.

MURDOCK WAS UP and moving before his alarm went off at four-thirty the next morning. He dressed in black jeans, a black T-shirt, his shoulder holster and a leather jacket. He pulled on his boots and strapped on his leather chaps. He'd leave the chaps at her clinic along with his motorcycle.

The cool mountain air whipped what lingering sleep might have clouded his mind, making his thoughts and mission crystal clear...to get Gabbie to her destination and back intact.

When he pulled in front of her clinic at five

o'clock, her truck was parked alongside the building, a horse trailer connected to the hitch.

Gabbie stood at the open barn door. "You can park your motorcycle inside." She tilted her head to the side. "Unless you want to take it with us."

He glanced at the horse trailer.

She stepped out of the building and crossed to the trailer. "It's big enough to carry four horses with gates inside that can separate each." She turned to him. "We're only taking one horse, which would leave room for your bike."

He frowned, his gut knotting, telling him their simple drop-off would be anything but simple. "Let's do it."

Gabbie dropped the ramp at the rear of the trailer, and Murdock rolled his motorcycle into the front compartment.

Gabbie handed him a tie-down strap and, armed with another, he went to work securing the bike.

It didn't take long before the bike was secure and closed behind a partition.

Gabbie climbed into the driver's seat, and Murdock rode shotgun.

As she shifted into gear, she shot a glance his

way. "What? You're not going to insist on driving, are you?"

He shook his head. "I'm an equal-opportunity kind of guy. Besides, this way, you do what you do best, which is drive a truck towing a horse trailer. And I do what I do best, keep my hands free in case I need to shoot something." He grinned and settled back in his seat. "But seriously, if you need me to drive, I've driven trucks and towed trailers before. I just prefer to ride a motorcycle."

"Good to know," she said.

The drive out to the Double Diamond Ranch was accomplished in the dark and silence. The gate at the ranch was closed. Gabbie entered a code into a keypad, and it swung open.

"I take it you're familiar with this ranch?" Murdock commented.

Gabbie nodded. "I grew up riding horses with the foreman's daughter, Dezi Thomas. You might know her; she's the chef at the lodge."

Murdock nodded. "A damned good chef, at that. She and Grimm are an item."

"She seems happy, but then she's always been an optimist with the most positive attitude of anyone I've ever known," Gabbie said.

"She's good for him. Grimm's happier than I've

ever known him to be." Murdock chuckled. "That's saying a lot."

Gabbie drove past the ranch house and continued around the back to the barn. Lights shone on the outside corners of the barn and through the open barn door.

As soon as Gabbie pulled to a halt, a man emerged, leading a beautiful black stallion.

The horse pranced beside the man, his head held high, his silky mane and tail flowing in the breeze. He was magnificent.

"Wow," Murdock said.

"The Double Diamond breeds some of the best show horses in the country," Gabbie said. "That stallion is from a champion bloodline and worth more than $100,000. He'll probably show for a couple of years and then be used as a stud."

Murdock let out a long, low whistle. "Maybe we should have a squad of protectors along on this ride."

"Gabbie," the man leading the horse approached.

"Good morning, Mr. Thomas," Gabbie shook Mr. Thomas's hand. She waved a hand toward Murdock. "Sean Murdock is riding shotgun. He's on loan from Hank Patterson's Brotherhood

Protectors. Murdock, this is Dan Thomas, the foreman of the Double Diamond."

Mr. Thomas shook Murdock's hand. "I'm glad you're going with her. I'd go myself, but one of our mares is in labor. I need to stay with her until she delivers."

Gabbie frowned. "Want me to look her over before we leave?"

The foreman shook his head. "I don't expect any trouble. I like to be around just in case."

"I'll be back as soon as we deliver," Gabbie said. "Let me know if I need to stop by on my return."

"Will do," Thomas said.

Gabbie turned to the stallion. "Is he ready?"

"All cleaned up and pretty for his new owner." Mr. Thomas handed Gabbie the lead. "We prefer to do the delivery, but Mr. Howard insisted that a licensed veterinarian make sure the stallion made it to his destination safely. I'll be right back with the bill of sale and medical records." The foreman ducked back into the barn.

Gabbie led the stallion to the trailer.

Murdock hurried ahead, lowered the ramp and stood back as she approached.

The stallion stopped short of the ramp and refused to go another step, tossing his head repeatedly, half-lifting Gabbie off the ground each time.

She stood her ground and spoke calmly, rubbing his neck and scratching behind his ears.

When the horse stopped jerking his head, she urged him forward a little at a time until his front hooves landed on the ramp.

He hesitated.

Gabbie continued speaking in a soft, soothing tone, led him up the ramp into the trailer and tied his lead to a hook on the wall. She patted his neck and stepped aside to close the gate that would keep him confined to a narrow space, giving him less opportunity to injure himself.

"I'm impressed," Murdock said as Gabbie stepped off the ramp. "I feel like I should call you the horse whisperer." He raised the ramp and locked it in place.

"He just needed a little reassurance," she said.

"They train their horses to trailer easily." Gabbie walked around the side of the trailer and met the foreman beside her truck.

He handed her a glossy black folder with the Double Diamond logo emblazoned on the cover. "All the documents are enclosed. Have him sign the copy on top acknowledging the delivery. Keep it and give him the rest. I'll come by your office to pick up our copy, so you don't have to drive back out here if we don't need you with the mare."

"Got it," Gabbie said. Then she leaned up and hugged the man's neck. "It's good to see you. I love that Dezi is back in town. We have to do lunch together at the lodge soon."

The foreman smiled down at her. "I'd like that. Let me know when you're not galivanting around the county long enough to sit down for a meal."

"I will." She smiled and waved.

Mr. Thomas's brow dipped low. "Be careful out there."

"Don't worry. I'll make sure he gets there in one piece," she promised.

"I'm not so much worried about the horse as I am about you. There are some crazy people out there."

Gabbie nodded toward Murdock. "I have backup."

"I'll bring her back safely," Murdock said.

The foreman's eyes narrowed. "See that you do. Our Gabbie is special."

Of that, Murdock couldn't agree more.

With the horse loaded and their destination programmed into the map function on his cell phone, Murdock sat back in his seat and stared at the highway ahead.

They drove the winding roads out of the Crazy Mountains, across the flatlands leading into Bozeman with its backdrop of snowcapped peaks. Out the other side of Bozeman, they headed toward Butte.

Murdock commented on the scenery and kept the conversation to a minimum, sensing Gabbie's concern and focus on making the trip as smooth and uneventful as possible.

"We'll fuel up at the truck stop in Butte. That will give me a chance to check on the horse, and we can grab something to eat," Gabbie said as they passed a sign indicating the distance to the next town. She glanced his way. "Are you doing all right?"

He smiled. "I should be asking you that question." Murdock's gaze fell on her hands gripping the steering wheel. "You've white-knuckled for the past thirty minutes."

Gabbie looked down at her hands and sighed. She raised her right hand and shook it as if to get the blood flowing. "The closer we get to Last Resort, the more uneasy I get."

"I'd say everything is going to be just fine..."

She shot a glance his way. "But?"

He shrugged. "My gut's telling me it won't be as simple as we'd like it to be."

"Then lie to me and tell me everything will be just fine." She laughed, the sound a little high-pitched and nervous.

"Okay. Everything is going to be just fine." His gut was telling him a different story. Like Gabbie, the closer they got to Last Resort, the more he was convinced things would go south.

He reached for her right hand and took it in both of his, rubbing the blood back into her fingers. "Whatever happens, I'm here to protect you."

"I'm not worried about me," she said. "I'm worried about the $100,000 worth of horse in the trailer. I'll feel better when he's safely delivered. Until then, I'll be a nervous wreck." She smiled at him. "But that feels good. Don't stop."

He continued to massage her hand, liking how slender and strong her fingers were. Her nails were cut short, but they were clean, and her hands bore calluses from working hard. Gabbie wasn't a girlie-girl.

She cast a twisted smile in his direction. "You don't have to keep doing that."

"I'll stop if you want me to," he said.

"I kind of like it, although I'm self-conscious about how masculine my hands are."

"I think they're beautiful, feminine and capable." He raised her hand to his lips and brushed a kiss across her knuckles.

She laughed. "Is that like saying an ugly girl has a great personality?"

"Not in my books. You're a different kind of beautiful."

Her brow furrowed. "Definitely the ugly girl with a great personality syndrome."

"Seriously, you have no idea how sexy and beautiful you are."

"Now I know you're lying. There's nothing sexy about red hair and freckles. I'm built like a boy, and I don't bother to wear makeup or pretty clothes."

"Stop." Murdock frowned at her. "I've dated girls who are pretty on the outside but empty on the inside."

When she opened her mouth, he squeezed her hand. "Let me finish."

She sighed. "I'm a captive audience. I'm not going anywhere."

"I see a fiery, fierce woman with a heart of gold

and hands that can soothe even the wildest beast. You don't need makeup or fancy clothes. Your beauty lies in your simplicity and openness."

She snorted. "That's right. What you see is what you get."

"Exactly," he said and smiled. "You're so real that I find it refreshing and exciting. When I saw you flying across the ground on the back of that black mare, I envied the complete connection you had with the horse, with the wind and with the sun glinting off your hair and skin. Sweetheart, you're amazing, sexy and beautiful just the way you are."

She stared at the road ahead, her eyes glistening. "No one has ever called me beautiful."

"Then shame on them. It's as plain as the freckles on your face and the sunshine in your hair."

A single tear slipped down her cheek. He released her hand and reached up to brush the tear away. "I'm sorry," he said. "I didn't mean to make you cry."

"I don't cry." She sniffed, and her eyes rounded. "Damn, this is our exit." She hit the turn signal and slowed to take the exit toward Butte.

Murdock would have said more, but he didn't want to disturb her concentration as she maneuvered the truck and trailer off the highway and into the truck stop, opting to top off where the eighteen-wheelers pumped their diesel fuel.

Murdock dropped down from the truck and managed the fuel pump while Gabbie checked on the stallion and gave the trailer a quick inspection, checking the hitch, tires and door latches.

She moved with the smooth grace of someone who was completely natural and unaware of her allure.

Some men would think she was too manly because she could do anything a male could do and probably do it better.

Murdock liked that she was strong, independent and capable. Hell, she worked with horses so much bigger and stronger than she was, unafraid and charmingly gentle.

"I'm going inside to use the facilities. I won't be long. I was going to grab a breakfast sandwich or something like it. Do you want one?" she asked.

"Yes, thank you," he said. "I'll keep an eye on the horse and trailer."

"Thank you." Gabbie spun on her boot heels and hurried into the station.

Murdock finished pumping the diesel and replaced the nozzle on the pump. When he turned to fit the cap on the tank, he thought he heard a muffled voice calling out from inside of something.

He walked the length of the truck and trailer, straining to hear the sound again.

The roar of diesel engines and the screech of trucks braking drowned out most sounds. As he passed the window into the stallion's stall, he stopped and listened again.

The horse stomped his hoof against the trailer floor, the thumping sound continuing as if in an echo from a tractor-trailer rig twenty feet away.

The thumping sounded again, but not from the horse trailer at all.

"Hey, Murdock, I brought you a sausage and egg biscuit and a cup of black coffee," Gabbie called out. "Where are you?"

"At the back of the trailer," he answered, straining to catch the thumping sound again.

Gabbie joined him, carrying a brown paper bag. "I left the coffee in the cup holders in the truck. Are you ready to go, or do you need to visit the facilities?"

He held a finger to his lips. "I thought I heard something."

Gabbie's brow wrinkled as she spun toward the

horse trailer. "Is everything all right with the stallion?"

Murdock nodded. "The sound wasn't coming from this trailer." He nodded toward the row of trailers parked behind the fueling area.

The thumping sounded again.

"There," he said. "Did you hear that?"

She frowned. "It's coming from one of those trailers." Gabbie started toward the trailers.

Murdock caught up with her as she reached the closest trailer to them.

Thumping sounded again. This time, Murdock could swear he heard a muffled voice calling out.

"It's coming from that one." Gabbie pointed to the third trailer in line.

As they neared the trailer, the thumping and the muffled voice grew louder.

Gabbie and Murdock stopped next to the trailer.

"Hello?" Gabbie said aloud.

The thumping stopped, and silence fell on the trailer.

Gabbie looked at Murdock and then back to the trailer. "Can you hear me?"

"Yes, oh yes," the voice said, breaking on what sounded like a sob. "Please. Help. Me."

CHAPTER 4

GABBIE LAID a hand on the trailer as if she could feel the person's hand through the metal side. "Are you hurt?"

"No." The girl's voice came through shaky. "I'm trapped. Please, get me out."

Murdock rushed to the rear of the trailer and poked his head around the corner. "It's got a lock on it."

"We'll have to find the truck driver to have him unlock the door," Gabbie said.

"No!" the small voice said. "You can't let anyone know. Please. Get me out."

Murdock joined Gabbie. "It's a combination lock."

"I think it's a girl," Gabbie whispered. "We have

to get her out of there. I have bolt cutters behind the back seat in my truck."

"I'll get them. Stay with her." Murdock left Gabbie and ran back to the truck.

Gabbie moved closer to the trailer, staying in the shadows. She glanced around, looking for anyone headed their way. If someone had locked the girl in the trailer, he might return before they got her out and moved her to a safe location.

"Talk to me," Gabbie spoke softly. "What's your name?"

"Lyssa," she said. "Lyssa Reinhart. Please, get me out. I have to get away from here."

"Why?" Gabbie asked.

"I can't let them find me," she said, her voice trailing off. "I can't go back. I'd rather die."

The desperation in her tone ripped at Gabbie's heart. "Lyssa, you're going to be all right. We'll help. Just hang in there."

"Please, please, get me out of here," she sobbed.

"We will, sweetie," Gabbie promised. "We have to cut the lock off the back of the trailer." Out of the corner of her eye, she spotted Murdock hurrying toward her, carrying the bolt cutters.

"Thank God," she murmured.

As he passed the first trailer, he stopped and

ducked into the shadows. Pressing a finger to his lips, his gaze met Gabbie's.

Gabbie whispered to the girl. "Be quiet. Someone's coming."

A muffled sob sounded from inside the trailer, and then silence.

Dropping to her haunches, Gabbie slipped into the shadows beneath the trailer.

Footsteps crunched on the gravel parking lot.

A man appeared at the end of the trailer. He slowed for a moment, dropped a lit cigarette to the ground and smashed it with his boot. He remained in that spot for a long moment, blowing a stream of smoke from his lips.

Gabbie held her breath, praying the man didn't hop into the truck's cab and drive off with the girl trapped inside.

Just when Gabbie thought she'd have to knock the man out, he moved, continuing past her trailer and the next one down the line.

Gabbie followed his legs until he turned at the fifth rig.

She let go of the breath she'd held and slipped out from beneath the trailer.

A moment later, Murdock joined her, his footsteps barely registering, even if the loose gravel. "Keep an eye out while I cut the lock."

She nodded, positioned herself at the corner of the next trailer and studied the light and shadows leading toward the station.

Behind her, a loud metallic snap sounded. She glanced back to see Murdock slip the lock from the hasp. He quickly shifted the levers holding the door closed and pulled the right side open.

A girl with sandy blond hair tumbled out into Murdock's arms. Immediately, she fought to free herself from his hold. "No," she cried. "Let me go. I'm not going back."

"Let me." Gabbie reached for the girl.

Murdock only released her when Gabbie had a firm hold.

Lyssa fell against Gabbie, sobs shaking her slim body.

"Shhh," Gabbie soothed, stroking the teen's tangled hair. "You're going to be all right."

"No. It's not over." She lifted her head, her gaze darting left and right. "They'll be looking for me. I'll never be safe from them, nor will the others."

Murdock touched Gabbie's shoulder. "We should move away from the truck. The driver could return at any moment."

Gabbi curled her arm around Lyssa's shoulders and guided her away from the line of tractor-trailer rigs and toward her truck and the horse trailer.

Once there, she turned to face the girl. "Lyssa, who can we call for you? Your parents? A grandparent, guardian or the police?"

Lyssa shook her head. "My parents are dead. It was just me and my four-year-old sister when they stole us from our foster family."

"You were in foster care?" Gabbie asked.

The girl's lips thinned. "I'm only fifteen. They wouldn't let me raise my younger sister on my own. So, they handed us over to child welfare and stuck us in a foster home." Her mouth twisted. "I should've been content since they kept me and my sister, Samantha, together in one home. I didn't know we had it good…until we were taken from our bus stop, a block from our foster home."

Gabbie frowned. "Who stole you?"

Lyssa looked up into Gabbie's eyes. "Followers of TCW."

Murdock frowned. "TCW? What's TCW?"

"The Chosen Way," Lyssa answered, her lip curling into an angry snarl. "They're horrible."

"Can you elaborate with names?" Murdock pressed.

Lyssa pinched the bridge of her nose and closed her eyes. "Bodie Vance grabbed me. His slimeball partner took my sister. We were gagged, tied and transported in the back of a van to their compound, run by a man called Cain Morgan."

Gabbie frowned when she didn't recognize any of the names Lyssa mentioned.

"Us girls were kept in a metal building with no running water or toilets. Lethal Linda was in charge of corralling the girls. I don't know her real name. She was mean and yelled at us all the time. I have bruises on my arms where she pinched me if I didn't do exactly what she wanted." Lyssa rubbed her hand up and down her left arm, wincing with each pass.

Gabbie reached for Lyssa's arm. The trail of small purple and yellow bruises gave testimony to the girl's story.

Gabbie's gut clenched and anger simmered beneath the calm surface she portrayed. "You said girls?"

The teen nodded. "Ten of us. Some as young as my sister and others as old as seventeen. When Sam and I arrived, there were only five of us.

Within a week, we were up to ten." She stared out the front windshield. "After talking among the others, we learned that we all came from either foster care or single-parent homes. None of the families could afford much. Certainly not a private investigator to find their missing girls. No one came to the compound looking for any of us." Her eyes rounded, and a tear slipped from one corner.

Gabbie's heart squeezed hard at the devastation in the teen's face.

Murdock stared into the side mirror and stiffened. "We need to get moving. The truck driver just got back to his rig." The Navy SEAL shifted into drive and pulled through the row of fuel pumps to the other side of the sprawling truck stop.

"Did the people of TCW put you into the back of that truck?" Gabbie asked.

Lyssa shook her head. "No. The other girls helped me slip out of the compound in the middle of the night. I promised to get away and come back with help." Her face crumpled. "I had to leave Sam. She'll be devastated. I walked through the night, following the highway into Anaconda, where I hitched a ride by sneaking into the back of a pickup truck." She hugged herself around her middle. "I've never been that cold in my life. The truck stopped here. I got out and slipped into the back of that trailer, hoping it would leave soon and take me further away from the compound. The next thing I knew, the driver had snapped a lock on the door, and I was trapped."

"Why didn't you go inside the station and ask for help?" Gabbie asked.

Lyssa shook her head, her eyes widening. "I heard some TCW men talking about their jobs in Butte. I couldn't risk it. One of the station workers could be a member of TCW."

Murdock shot a quick glance toward Lyssa. "What about the police or sheriff's department?"

Again, Lyssa shook her head. "We saw a sheriff's truck in the compound one day. He was bringing one of the boys who'd escaped back to the compound. I don't know how far their network reaches. I needed to get far enough away before I could trust someone to help me. And the sooner, the better." Her bottom lip trembled. "I promised my sister we'd stick together. She'll think…" Her voice caught on a sob. "She'll think I left her. That I didn't care. She has no one there to defend her."

Gabbie held the girl's hand. "We'll help." She

looked across the console to Murdock. "Won't we?"

He nodded. "Damn right, we will."

"Thing is…if you send in a bunch of police, the TCW has escape plans. They can disappear into the mountains with all their captives. Then Sam will be lost forever." Lyssa shook her head. "You can't do that." She wrung her hands, her face puckering for another flood of tears. "It's hopeless. You can't get into the area without someone to vouch for you. They're scaring people off by firing guns in the air and discouraging people from stopping even long enough to fill their gas tanks."

"If you've been confined to the compound, how do you know all this?"

Lyssa's lips tipped upward. "I listen."

"Why didn't you send one of the other girls instead of undertaking this journey yourself?" Murdock asked.

Lyssa's eyes narrowed. "None of them had the balls to step up to the task. It was up to me to escape or continue to be a prisoner with no hope of getting out or shutting down whatever plans they have for us." She looked from Gabbie to Murdock and back to Gabbie. "Please tell me you're not a part of TCW." She crossed her fingers and bit her bottom lip, fear radiating from every pore of her body.

Gabbie touched the girl's arm. "You're okay. We're not members of TCW. I'm Gabbie Myers, a veterinarian tasked with delivering a horse to a ranch on the other side of Last Resort."

Lyssa shook her head. "You can't go there. That's where the TCW compound is. Well, just outside of town. From what I've overheard eavesdropping on Linda and Bodie, the residents of Last Resort are either members or are gone. They drove out anyone who disagreed with them."

Gabbie's lips pressed together. TCW sounded like a dangerous organization. "I came with back-up." She nodded toward Murdock. "Our driver is Sean Murdock, prior military, Navy SEAL and my protector for this mission."

Lyssa's eyes widened. "Protector? Wow. My sister could use one right now."

"Any idea what TCW plans to do with the children they've captured?" Murdock asked.

Lyssa's eyes narrowed. "No. But they're short on cash and are planning on increasing their supply of ammunition and explosives. The older girls and I think they're planning some kind of attack. We figure they'll either sell the girls to get the money they need to supply the attack or train us to join their cause. We've seen them working with the boys, putting them through something like army training, teaching them how to shoot guns and throw grenades."

Gabbie marveled at how calm Lyssa was when stating her hypothesis. Considering the most plausible option was human trafficking for money to fund their event, the girls could be shuffled off to the highest bidder and live miserable lives as potentially drugged prostitutes. "We can't let either option happen," Gabbie said.

Lyssa chewed on her bottom lip for a moment and then shook her head. "Unless you have an army, you can call on or a secret weapon that will annihilate all of the members of TCW, I don't think you can stop them."

Gabbie smiled. "We have a valid reason to be near Last Resort."

Murdock tipped his head. "The horse in the trailer behind us."

"That's right," Gabbie said. "Surely the local billionaire has some pull with TCW and can get us safe passage into and out of Last Resort, especially if we 'accidentally' stumble on the compound and claim it's where the directions for delivery led us."

Murdock leaned forward. "We'll need you to tell us everything you can remember about the compound."

"I can do that," Lyssa said. "When I realized we weren't going to be rescued, I studied the layout and where they positioned guards. I got a pretty good idea of what was in most of the buildings."

"I'll need to get Hank on the phone. He'll have to send someone out here to collect Lyssa before we can go in."

Lyssa frowned. "I'm going with you."

"No," Gabbie and Murdock spoke as one.

"But I know my way around," she argued. "I can get you where you want to go quickly. I know where they're keeping the girls. Where Sam is."

"You can draw a diagram of the compound," Murdock suggested. "We'll find the girls and get them out."

"What about the boys?" Lyssa shook her head. "They might think you're just another TCW adult, there to make their lives miserable."

Gabbie shook her head. "We can't risk your recapture."

Lyssa gripped Gabbie's hand. "Sam's my sister. I should be there for her."

"You've done your part," Murdock said. "We'll

take it from here. If we have to call in for backup, we will. But we can't take you in. If they see you, it'll blow our cover. Then no one will get out."

Lyssa stared at Murdock, her eyes narrowing. "It won't blow your cover if you take me back, returning me to the TCW compound like the sheriff who brought back the boy who got away." Her eyes widened. "That way, I can get inside to the others and tell them to be ready when you figure out how to free them."

Gabbie held up her hands. "No. Absolutely not. You're free. We want to make sure you stay that way, safe and out of reach of that."

Lyssa's brow lowered in a fierce frown.

Before she could open her mouth to protest, Murdock faced her, his gaze intent, his jaw rock solid.

Gabbie's heart turned cartwheels. Even stern, the man made her breath catch, and her body sit up and take notice.

His look softened. "Those people are armed. We don't know what will set them off."

Lyssa's chin lifted. "All the more reason I need to be with Samantha when the shit hits the fan. She's only four and has no clue what to do when someone goes on a shooting rampage."

"And you do?" Murdock challenged,

Lyssa snorted. "It's standard training for all school-aged children these days."

It made Gabbie sad that the teen was correct. "With the number of mass shootings at public schools that have taken place in the past decade, it makes sense to train teachers and children to protect themselves in such a situation."

Murdock sighed. "So, you've had mass shooter training. This is different. How many people are in this TCW group?"

Lyssa shook her head. "They had what they called a town meeting one night. We were marching from the dining hall to our metal building when Cain gave his speech. There had to be a hundred people gathered around. All of them were armed with some kind of gun. Some of them wore those bullet-proof vests the soldiers wear in battle. Cain was giving them a pep talk or a call to arms or something. He'd say something, and they'd shout a response." Lyssa shivered. "It was like they were under his spell."

"Brainwashed," Gabby said.

"Yeah," Lyssa leaned forward. "It was frightening. Sam had nightmares that night. I held her until morning. That's when I decided I had to do it. I had to get out and get help."

"We'll do our best to get in, assess the situation and come up with a plan to rescue the children," Murdock said. "But we can't make any promises. We might have to regroup and bring in more people to make it happen."

"They're planning something," Lyssa said. "I'm afraid the children will disappear if we wait too long."

Gabbie stared into Murdock's gaze, her mind churning with different scenarios, each worse than the one before. "We need backup."

Murdock nodded. "First and foremost, we need someone to infiltrate and monitor movement into and out of the compound at all times. Hank's team was pretty tapped out with their current assignments." A grin lifted the corners of his mouth. "My team, on the other hand, is on hiatus until more supplies arrive at the lodge." He had his cell phone out and was dialing before he finished the sentence.

"Drake, Murdock here. We have a situation." For the next few minutes, he filled in his teammate on their encounter with Lyssa in the truck stop parking lot and her story about the other children who'd been kidnapped and were now being held for some nefarious purpose that could only be bad.

"Thanks. I'll share my cell phone location with you so you can always find me." Murdock snorted. "True. Wherever there's reception. Touch base with Hank and Swede and let them know what's happening. They can track Gabbie on their computer. They might also have suggestions for how to infiltrate and get the kids out without starting a war." He listened for a moment and nodded. "We'll drop a pin and wait for you to catch up."

Gabbie touched his arm and tipped her head toward the teen sharing her seat.

Murdock nodded. "Most importantly, someone will need to escort Lyssa to a safe location until we can reunite her with her little sister."

Lyssa crossed her arms over her chest, her lips pressing together in a straight line. "I'm going with you."

"Out here." Murdock ended the call and slid his cell phone back into his pocket. "No. You're not. We'll be too worried about you to focus on the mission. It's better for you and us if you stay behind." He held up his hand when Lyssa opened her mouth to argue. "This is not negotiable. And I need you to get into the backseat and make your-self invisible."

Lyssa closed her mouth and slipped between the two front seats, landing in the backseat, where she pulled a loose blanket over her head and shoul-ders and hunkered down in a corner. Throughout her move, the stubborn look remained on her face.

Gabbie knew that look from when she'd been growing up and had been told she couldn't do something. She'd taken the word *no* as a challenge and found a way to do it anyway.

Lyssa had been through enough already. She needed to leave the rest to the men trained to rescue and extract individuals from impossible locations and situations.

For now, they had to wait for Murdock's team to converge on their location. While they waited, they'd have to keep a close eye on the teen until they handed her off to one of Murdock's men.

CHAPTER 5

WITH A COUPLE of hours to kill, Murdock parked, went back into the truck stop, loaded up on sandwiches, chips and drinks and returned to the truck.

Gabbie stood beside the driver's door. "If you don't mind, I'll drive."

"Please," he said and rounded the hood to the other side. "Our mutual friend made a good point," he said as he climbed into the passenger seat and closed the door before he continued. "If some of the TCW men work in Butte, it will only be a matter of time before they notice the truck and horse trailer parked for a couple of hours at the truck stop. Rather than draw attention to us sitting in one place so long, we should find a nearby park, have lunch and maybe let the horse out for a few minutes to stretch his legs."

Gabbie grinned. "I was going to suggest the same thing." She slid into the driver's seat and closed her door.

Murdock climbed into the passenger seat and laid the bags of food on the console. After he buckled his seatbelt, he pulled out his cell phone and searched for a nearby park. "There's an open area recreational space on the northwest corner of town. It's in the direction we're heading but off the main highway." He selected the park and brought up the directions.

Gabbie pulled out onto the highway, heading west.

The town of Butte had almost thirty-five thousand residents. Murdock hoped not all of those residents were members of TCW. To be on the safe side and avoid being spotted, he made sure Lyssa remained in the truck. The tinted windows made it impossible for people outside Gabbie's vehicle to see clearly into the backseat.

Before exiting the vehicle, he handed the teen a sandwich, a bag of chips and a canned soft drink. "Enjoy," he called out as he snagged the bag with the remaining sandwiches and an old quilt from the back seat.

Casting a glance around, Murdock sighed. "Seems a shame to spend a sunny day wedged into the backseat corner."

"I don't mind," Lyssa said. "Beats lying in the back of an old ranch truck, shivering so hard, my fingers got numb and my teeth rattled."

Murdock stared around the interior of the cab and then turned to Gabbie. "Do you have a piece of paper and something to write with?"

"Maybe." Gabbie reached into the glove box and pulled out a folded paper detailing an oil and filter change. She fished out a pen and turned to Lyssa. "While you're eating, we need you to draw what you remember about the compound and surrounding area."

Lyssa lifted her wrapped sandwich to her nose and sniffed. "Umm. This sandwich smells delicious. I haven't eaten anything since they fed us bologna sandwiches for lunch yesterday."

"My stomach is already growling." Gabbie pressed a hand to her flat belly.

"Bologna?" Murdoch laughed. He loved a good bologna sandwich with mustard slathered across the bread. "To this day, when I want comfort food…a bologna sandwich is right up there with chicken soup."

Gabbie grimaced. "Not for me. My mother packed bologna sandwiches in my lunchbox every day when I was in grade school." She laughed. "I still can't face bologna and gag if I smell it anywhere in the house."

Lyssa stared down at her sandwich without taking a bite. "I'd eat a bologna sandwich every day if it meant my mother was still here and had made it for me. I'd give anything to have her back."

Gabbie laid a hand on Lyssa's arm. "I'm so sorry for your loss. How did she die?" She held up her hand. "You don't have to say if it's still too painful."

Lyssa shook her head. "It's okay. I've learned to keep my grief hidden or only let it out when no one's looking." Still holding her sandwich, she stared down at the thickly sliced bread. "My father crashed his car into a utility pole driving too fast on an icy road over a year ago. It was right after my mother was diagnosed with Stage 4 breast cancer that had metastasized before they caught it. She went to the doctor because she wasn't feeling good." Lyssa sighed. "She thought it was the flu. When the doctor referred her to an oncologist, she was confused. Then scared."

"I can't imagine how terrifying that was," Gabbie said.

"It was horrible," Lyssa whispered. "I went with her when the doctor gave her the news that she had terminal cancer."

"So young to carry that burden," Gabbie said.

"Too young," Murdoch added, his chest tightening.

"She was dying but was more worried about what would happen to us. I kept assuring her that we'd be all right. I'd make sure Samantha didn't lack love and attention." Lyssa moved her head slowly, side to side. "I've failed my mother and my little sister."

"No, you haven't," Gabbie said. "You got away, and we found you. You were doing the right thing by getting help."

"Gabbie's right," Murdock said. "We'll see that you're reunited with your sister."

"And that you both find a safe place to live together," Gabbie added. "Now, eat that sandwich. You have to keep up your strength for when you see your sister again."

"I know. I can't ever quit. Sam and I only have each other now. She needs me. And I sure as hell need her."

"Eat," Murdock said. "We'll work on that map when we're done." He took the food bag from Gabbie's arm and dug out a sandwich.

Gabbie took the quilt from Murdock and looped it over her arm. "We won't wander too far. We'll just get out on the grass a few feet away. If anyone drives by, all they'll see is a couple stopping for a picnic," she assured Lyssa. "If you get into any trouble, all you have to do is yell. One of us, or both, will be right here for you."

"Thank you, Gabbie," Lyssa gave her a watery smile. "It feels good knowing I'm not alone."

Gabbie carried the blanket to a grassy spot several feet from the truck and spread it out on the ground. She dropped onto the soft fabric and frowned toward the truck, her stomach rumbling louder with each passing minute.

Murdock joined her with the food and handed her the bag.

She pulled out a sandwich and peeled back a thin layer of paper wrapped around it. "Do you still have your parents?"

Murdock shook his head. "No. They passed while I was in BUD/s training over a decade ago. They'd come down with the flu and waited too long to see a doctor. By then, they had severe cases of pneumonia. From diagnosis to death was less than two weeks. I couldn't get out of training to see them before they died or even to attend their funerals."

"That's so hard. You had no closure," she murmured. "I'm so sorry."

"What about you?" he asked.

"I almost feel guilty." She gave him a crooked smile. "My folks are alive and kicking up their heels in the Florida sunshine."

"I'm glad for you," Murdock said. "I would love to have seen my parents one last time to say all the things I needed to say. Their deaths nearly flatlined my training. I couldn't focus and found myself wishing I could just walk away."

"But you didn't."

He shook his head. "I couldn't quit. My mother and father were beyond excited when I got into the program. I had to make it through. For them as much as for me. From then on, I regained my focus and worked through pain and exhaustion, making it through Hell Week and the last weeks of my training. You could say that my parents' death got me through BUD/s." He chuckled. "It's ironic that you feel guilty because yours are alive. I feel guilty because it took mine dying to motivate me to survive training and multiple deployments."

"Losing someone you love leaves a hole in your heart and your life," Gabbie said.

"Who have you lost?" Murdock asked.

Gabbie stared into the distance. "A dear friend, Penny Baker."

"Cancer?"

Gabbie shook her head. "Worse. She was on her way back to Montana from LA, having broken up with her boyfriend."

"What happened to her?" Murdock asked.

"We don't know." Gabbie raised her hands, palms up with a shrug. "She just disappeared. It's the worst feeling, not knowing. I almost wish we could find her body." She sighed. "Then again, maybe she's out there somewhere alive, waiting for us to rescue her."

"Were there no clues?" he asked.

"We were able to determine that she'd made it to Montana. Strangely, we found an item of her clothing in an abandoned mine. She's lost, and we haven't been able to find her."

Murdock took her hand and squeezed it gently.

Gabbie turned her hand into his and squeezed back. She glanced toward the truck. "Those little girls lost their mother and were stolen away from their school bus stop for what?"

"I hate to think what their abductors have in mind. It can't be good. Whatever it is, we won't let it happen."

"Agreed," Gabbie said.

Murdock quickly finished his sandwich and washed it down with a soda.

Gabbie didn't waste any time and choked down her sandwich. When she was finished, she looked toward the truck. "Let's see what Lyssa's come up with."

Murdock pushed to his feet and held out a hand to Gabbie.

She placed her palm in his and let him drag her upright.

He must have tugged a little harder than necessary. Gabbie tipped forward, stumbled and fell against Murdock's chest.

His arms came up around her, steadying her. "Better?" She still stood so close he could feel her warmth through the thin fabric of her blouse and his T-shirt.

Murdock brushed his knuckle across her cheek. Her skin was as soft and silky as he'd imagined. The more he was with her, the more he wanted to be. It was like a fixation or obsession he couldn't shake free of.

He looked down into her face, studying every curve and shadow. For the first time, he noted that she had green eyes to go along with all the thick red hair curling around her cheeks.

Her tongue darted out to moisten her lips, her gaze unwavering until it shifted from his eyes to his mouth.

Murdock groaned. Now was not the moment to find himself attracted to a female, no matter how incredibly perfect she was. The timing could have been better. But how much time did it take to steal a kiss? Hardly any at all.

His head lowered until his lips hovered over hers. "I don't know why, but I have this intense desire to kiss you."

Gabbie laughed; the sound was breathy and soft. "What's holding you back?"

"Nothing," he said and crushed her to him, claiming her mouth in a long, deep kiss that stole his breath away and left him longing for more than just that one kiss.

When he raised his head, he stared into her glazed green eyes, his heart lighter than it had been since before he'd signed on as a Navy SEAL.

This was a woman he could see himself spending a lifetime getting to know. A woman who was as real as the earth and beautiful in her subtle, very grounded way. If he wasn't careful, he could fall in love with her. He suspected he was halfway there already. And after only a day of knowing her.

She stared up at him, her eyes wide, her breathing ragged. "What's happening?" she whispered.

He laughed and pulled her closer, brushing his lips across hers before setting her at arm's length. "You've been kissed," he said. "I can't take it back, even if you want me to."

She raised her fingers to her lips and pressed her other hand to her heart. "I feel lightheaded and energized all at once. It's so strange."

Murdock's brow dipped. "Gabbie, you're a beautiful woman. Have you never been kissed before?"

She shook her head. "Not like that. I think you stole my breath away. Should I feel this way?"

"Absolutely." He chuckled softly and brushed a strand of her hair behind her ear. "Does it scare you?"

"A little. I've always been in control of my life,

until now. That kiss...made me feel as if I'd lost complete control. I'm not sure I like that feeling." She stepped closer and laid a hand on his chest. "Could you do it again?"

"For the sake of being sure," he said, a smile spreading across his face. He bent to claim her lips once again. This time, he started slow and gentle, exploring her lips before he swept his tongue across the seam.

She opened to him, her tongue meeting his in a primal dance that came as natural as breathing. Her hands rose to encircle the back of his neck, dragging him closer, deepening their kiss until their bodies pressed tightly together and breathing wasn't an option.

When he finally raised his head, his pulse thundered through his veins, and his cock had hardened, pressing against the fabric of his jeans.

Movement out of the corner of his eye reminded him of where they were. He squeezed her arms once, then let go and stepped away before he forgot everything again and repeated that incredible kiss.

"If you two are finished sucking face, I've got something you need to see," Lyssa called out through the open back window of the pickup.

Gabbie blinked and shifted her gaze away from him and toward the teenager clearly visible through the open window. "We should see what she wants."

Murdock nodded and scooped up the blanket and the bag filled with sandwich wrappers. He hooked Gabbie's arm and steered her toward the truck.

They joined Lyssa on the back seat.

She'd filled the back of the page Gabbie had given her with squares, fence lines and a couple of hand-drawn trees.

For the next fifteen minutes, she described each square and rectangle on the paper, identifying what could be found in each, as far as she'd been able to determine.

Then she talked about what she'd encountered as she'd followed the road into and out of the compound. "I had to slip past a guard posted on the edge of camp near the building where the girls are kept. Then I sneaked around the two at the front gate. I stuck to the tree line all the way out to the highway, where another guard covered the gravel road leading into the compound." She glanced up. "After that, the roads were clear of TCW sentries. I was able to make good time getting to Last Resort and skirting the town. It took me longer to reach Anaconda, where I slipped into a truck stopped at a gas station."

Murdock folded the drawing in half and slipped it into his wallet. He glanced at the clock on his cell phone and straightened. "Drake and the gang should be rolling in at any moment."

"Did you give them this location?" Gabbie asked.

"I did." Murdock's cell phone vibrated in his pocket. He fished it out and smiled. "Murdock here."

"Pulling into Butte as we speak," his friend and teammate said. "We should arrive at your location in less than ten mikes."

Murdock ended the call and met Gabbie's gaze. "Are you ready to perform a reconnaissance mission, deliver a horse and rescue some children?"

Her brow wrinkled, and she laughed. "I'm not sure all of that is in my job description. Sounds like something you're more familiar with. But I'm game. Although, I'd really like to get this horse to his new home before any bullets start flying."

Murdock's brow lowered in a frown. "I'm thinking we have to brave the lion's den to get eyes on our target. Pretending we're lost might get us onto the compound. Having the horse with us still might get us off without any live rounds expended."

Gabbie chewed on her bottom lip. "That's an expensive animal to be using as a Trojan horse."

Murdock grinned. "That's exactly what it is. Only we're not going in this time to fight. We're on a stealth mission to gather intel."

Gabbie nodded. "We go in, look around and get out. Got it."

"Then we'll deliver the stallion and regroup with the team to come up with an extraction plan." He looked from Gabbie to Lyssa and back to Gabbie. "Let me reiterate… We aren't going in to smash the TCW and grab the girls. We can't. Not with just Gabbie and me in broad daylight. If things go south, we do our best to get out of there in one piece." He glanced at Gabbie. "You know, the more I think about this, the more I'm convinced you aren't the right person for this job."

Gabbie's jaw hardened. "You don't have a choice. I'm the one the buyer requested. Not you. You're not a veterinarian. He specifically requested a vet to accompany the stallion."

"I could tell him you got sick and couldn't make

it," Murdock said. The thought of Gabbie walking into a hotbed of trigger-happy preppers didn't give him any warm fuzzies.

"You're not getting rid of me. I'm all in. Besides, it's my truck and trailer." She glanced out the window and smiled tightly. "They're here. It's time to get this show on the road." Gabbie climbed down out of the truck.

Murdock followed, his mind racing, trying to think of a way to convince her she didn't need to go.

Taking an unarmed civilian with no combat experience into a hot zone was a bad idea, any way he looked at it.

Murdock's gut feeling was screaming that this operation was going to get fucked up.

Gabbie turned to face him and reached up to cup his cheek. "Relax. We've got this." She smiled, patted his face and turned to greet the rest of his team.

That sinking feeling in the pit of his belly got a whole lot worse.

Oh, boy. They were so screwed.

CHAPTER 6

GABBIE DIDN'T LIKE TAKING the stallion into the compound, but it was the best cover story available to them at the moment. It was imperative that they get inside and see what was going on. She'd just have to ensure they got the horse and delivered it to the buyer in one piece. The number one priority was to get those children to safety.

All the cocky bravado she'd displayed back in Butte had been nothing but a façade—a big fat lie to get Murdock to agree to take her into the compound.

The thought of four-year-old Samantha alone and afraid had every latent maternal instinct she never realized she had to come to a screaming head. She couldn't sit back and do nothing to free the child and reunite the sisters. And she couldn't ignore the other kids who'd been stolen from their homes and lives.

With Murdock close behind her, Gabbie hurried toward the broad-shouldered men climbing out of a dark SUV.

A tall man with black hair and blue eyes stopped in front of her. "You must be Gabbie."

She nodded. "I am."

Murdock stood beside her. "Gabbie, this is Drake Morgan. He and I served together in the Navy."

"Drake." She shook the man's hand, pleased that his grip was firm and his hands were calloused from good honest labor.

Murdock waved toward the man with sandy-blond hair and blue eyes, who came to stand beside Drake. Equally as tall as Drake, he held out his hand. "Michael Reaper."

Gabbie shook the man's hand. "Michael."

"We call him Grimm." A man with auburn hair and brown eyes nudged Grimm aside. "He's an Army puke."

Grimm shot an irritated glance at the man. "Former Delta Force."

"Current Demolition Man," the auburn-haired

man said. "Like the rest of us." He held out his hand. "Pierce Turner, Marine Force Recon."

Gabbie took his hand and gave it a firm shake.

"He goes by Utah," Grimm added. "Stands for uptight asshole."

"Don't listen to him," Utah said. "He joined the Army because the Marines wouldn't take him."

A man with dark hair graying at the temples pushed his way between the two men. "Utah's just jealous he couldn't be a Delta Force Operative." He held out his hand. "Joe Smith. The guys call me Judge. We hear you and our man Murdock have discovered a situation."

Gabbie nodded. "It's definitely more than the two of us could handle by ourselves. Thank you all for coming."

Drake looked over her shoulder toward the truck and horse trailer. "Where's the girl?"

"In the back seat of the truck, laying low," Murdock said.

"I touched base with Hank Patterson like you asked me to," Drake said. "He offered to pull some of his people from their assignments if we need more help. He met us in Eagle Rock with everything we might need in the way of communications equipment, weapons and ammunition."

Murdock grinned. "Have you been to the Brotherhood Protectors operations center?"

Drake nodded. "The man is ready for Armageddon with his arsenal of weapons and ammunition."

"Let's hope we don't have to put it all to use against this group of radical survivalists."

Murdock held up the diagram Lyssa had drawn. The team and Gabbie gathered around the SUV and went over the layout of the compound and the location of the captured children.

"And to complicate the scenario," Murdock's gaze shifted to the truck where the teenager hid in the back seat, "Lyssa said there were about a hundred people at their town meeting several nights ago, all armed and excited about something."

"A barn-raising?" Utah offered. "Or maybe a gun show?"

"Or they're staging a coup against the government," Grimm said.

"D.C. is a long way from Montana," Judge said. "Wouldn't they concentrate on something a little closer to home?"

"Whatever it is," Murdock said, "Lyssa said it

had them roused and ready to go whenever their leader gives them the word."

Drake pointed to the drawing. "There's only one road in. They have guards on the road and around the perimeter. If there are a hundred people in that compound, it could be tricky getting those kids out without being noticed."

"Not all of the members of their movement are living at the compound," Gabbie said. "According to Lyssa, many of them are scattered out in the nearby town of Last Resort and further out in Anaconda and even Butte."

"What you're telling us," Grimm said, "is that we can't trust anyone in the area."

Murdock nodded. "We don't know who is part of their group and who isn't. They purged all non-believers from Last Resort, and outsiders are discouraged to the point that they're shot at for even driving through on the state highway."

Judge snorted. "Sounds like a friendly bunch."

"So, what's the plan?" Utah asked.

"Gabbie and I will drive into the compound with the truck and horse trailer."

Drake was shaking his head before Murdock finished. "You won't get past the guard on the road."

"We'll be insistent that the buyer gave us that address and that we aren't leaving without personally delivering the horse into the hands of the buyer."

"Where do we fit in?" Drake asked.

"Two of you need to hang back here in Butte with Lyssa to keep her safe," Murdock said. "You might even want to transport her back to Eagle Rock and Hank's ranch. They can keep her safely away from any of The Chosen Way zealots who might come after her and use her as an example of what happens to those who attempt to escape."

"What about the other two?" Grimm asked.

"We need two of our guys to camp out in the woods near the compound to keep an eye on the place until we come up with a plan to extract the children." Murdoch touched his finger to the center of the drawing. "We need to know if they're moving the children or anything else."

"A stakeout," Drake concluded.

"Our eyes on the ground can ride with us." Murdock continued. "They can drop short of the road in and go cross-country on foot. Gabbie and I will cause enough of a disturbance to allow them to move into position undetected."

Drake frowned and shook his head. "If they

have guards on the road in, I just don't see you getting past that point."

Gabbie lifted her chin. "I can demand to speak with the foreman or owner of the compound."

Judge cocked an eyebrow. "If verbal negotiations fail?"

"I'll walk in on foot," Gabbie said. "I'll tell them that if they don't like it, they'll have to shoot me in the back. I'll also tell them to be aware that I gave my coordinates to the state police and let them know that if I don't call within an hour, to come looking for me there."

Murdock frowned. "On second thought, you should stay with Lyssa."

Gabbie met his stern expression with one of her own. "I'm not going back to Eagle Rock until I know those children are safe and Lyssa and her sister are reunited and safely out of the hands of The Chosen Way."

"While you two are working your way into the compound, Grimm and I can get close enough to provide cover if things get ugly," Drake said.

Gabbie smiled at Drake. "Perfect." She turned back to Murdock. "We'll have their support if we need it."

"Two armed men against an army of gunslinging zealots?" Murdock's frown deepened. "Maybe this isn't the best idea."

"It's the only one we have," Gabbie insisted. "They're not going to shoot a woman and her horse."

"They stole children and fired on vehicles passing through town on a state highway," Murdock pointed out.

Gabbie's chin rose another notch. "There are children who need us to take whatever measures necessary to free them from their captors." She crossed her arms over her chest. "It's my truck, my trailer, and the stallion is my responsibility. If you don't want to take me, I won't let you take my truck, trailer and horse as cover to get you inside the compound." She squared her shoulders. Not only that, I'd go without you."

Murdock's face flushed a ruddy red as he faced off with Gabbie.

"Look," Drake's voice cut through the thick air between Gabbie and Murdock, "whatever you decide, we need to move on it. If they do have a plan in the works, it could include moving those kids. We could use all the intel we can get to devise a plan to free those kids."

Murdock's eyes narrowed for another second

before he broke their staring competition. "Fine. We'll go with the original plan."

"We need to move the girl to the SUV," Drake said, "suit up with radio communication and get moving."

"I'll get Lyssa," Gabbie said.

"Show me what Hank gave you," Murdock said.

While Drake opened the hatch on the SUV, Gabbie turned back to her truck, bracing herself for resistance from the teen.

As she opened the rear door of her king cab pickup, Gabbie said, "Lyssa, I need you to go with Murdock's team and do whatever they say. They're going to keep you safe until we can figure this out."

The girl didn't respond. Gabbie figured she was still angry at having to stay behind.

Gabbie glanced across the bench seat to the gray blanket Lyssa had pulled over her head. "Don't be angry, sweetie. It's just too dangerous for you to go back to the compound. Lyssa, talk to me." She reached for the blanket and tugged gently. The blanket slipped to the floor, and Gabbie's heart skipped several beats.

The lump beneath the blanket wasn't the teen at all, but the army-green duffel bag full of the

ELLE JAMES

items Hank Patterson had equipped them with and Murdock had stowed on the floorboard.

"Murdock!" Gabbie cried out.

"What's wrong," the ex-Navy SEAL called out as he raced to her side.

The other members of his team weren't far behind him.

Gabbie stood back and motioned toward the back seat. "Lyssa's gone."

"Son of a bitch." Murdock dove into the space, tossed the duffel bag aside and even looked behind the seat.

"She's not in there," Gabbie said.

"No, but she left this." He emerged with a piece of the oil-change receipt. On the back was a note scribbled in the same ink as Lyssa had used on the drawing of the compound.

Gabbie leaned close to Murdock and read the teen's words aloud.

I have to go back. Samantha needs me.

"Sweet Jesus," Gabbie whispered. "She's going back to the compound." She spun away from the truck and searched the area around them. "We have to stop her. She can't have gotten far."

Gabbie and the five men spread out and combed the area surrounding the truck and trailer.

The recreational area was surrounded by trees with a network of hiking paths leading out in multiple directions.

"Stay here," Murdock urged Gabbie.

"But we have to find her," Gabbie argued.

"Let us look," Murdock said. "You have an expensive horse to look after."

"The stallion will be fine on his own. I want to help."

Murdock gripped her shoulders and stared down into her eyes. "If she changes her mind and comes back, it would be better if you're the one here for her."

Gabbie frowned. "I'd rather be actively searching."

"I know."

"Fine. I'll stay. But please, find her."

"We'll do our best." Murdock bent, brushed his lips across hers and spun away to the trail the other men hadn't gone down.

Gabbie returned to the truck and trailer, checked on the stallion and gave him water and a little grain. She'd packed the trailer with enough grain and hay for a three-day journey, though they'd only planned on it taking one.

She'd learned the hard way that anything could

happen when transporting animals across the country, no matter how short the distance. Weather, fires, traffic and more could delay them for hours and sometimes days.

The stallion drank the water, ate the feed, then stamped his hooves against the rubber mat covering the trailer floor.

Running her hand along his neck, Gabbie whispered, "I know. We should've dropped you off at your new home by now. But be patient, big guy. Just by being you, you'll help us find and free those children." She scratched behind the horse's ears and spoke in soothing tones until the horse stopped pawing at the floor and settled down.

Gabbie gave the stallion a section of hay from the loose bale stored in the front compartment where she'd customized the drawers and cabinets to hold a wide variety of medicine and equipment she might need on the visits she made to outlying ranches. Once the stallion was happily munching on the hay, Gabbie stepped out of the trailer and closed the door behind her.

She scanned the tree line, hoping to see Lyssa emerge, contrite and ready to cooperate. Instead of the girl, the men appeared one by one from the various trails.

Murdock was the last to step out of the shadows and join her at the truck. "I ran about a mile up my trail, hoping to catch up to her," he said.

"Same," Drake said. "When I turned around, I walked back more slowly, searching the woods just off the trail for any sign of the girl."

"I did the same," Utah said.

Grimm and Judge sounded off with the same effort.

"As much as I don't like leaving, knowing the girl is unaccounted for," Drake said, "you can't wait much longer to make your appearance at the compound."

"He's right," Murdock said. "We can't go after dark. They might be more inclined to shoot."

"Utah and I will stay here and look for the girl," Judge said. "We'll give it another hour at the least, expanding our search in an ever-widening grid."

Gabbie didn't want to leave without locating Lyssa first, but Murdock was right. "We have to go. We need to have enough time to make our appearance at the compound and then get on to the original reason for this trip."

"To deliver a horse." Murdock snorted. "So much for a simple job."

Gabbie turned to Judge and Utah. "When you find her, tell her we're going in and will do everything in our power to fix this."

Judge nodded. "We'll do our best to find and hold onto the young lady."

"Thank you. Oh, and you might check the truck stop. That's where we found her. She might have gone back, looking for a way to hitch a ride heading west."

"We'll look there next," Judge said.

Gabbie climbed into the driver's seat and waited for Murdock, Drake and Grimm to get in and close their doors.

Judge and Utah went back to their search for the missing teen.

Once the truck was loaded, Gabbie drove out of the recreation area and onto the highway heading west.

Gabbie blamed herself for leaving the teen alone. They should have kept her with them or in sight until they'd handed her over to Judge and Utah. Hell, she never expected the girl to take off.

Gabbie drove away from Butte, feeling awful that the troubled teen had slipped through their fingers and was on her own in a sometimes unforgiving world.

But she couldn't dwell on Lyssa. Not when they had a reconnaissance mission to accomplish and a plan to make to rescue some kids, including a four-year-old little girl named Samantha.

Gabbie passed through the small town of Anaconda, continuing west.

While she drove, the men in the backseat slid radio headsets over their ears and checked to ensure they functioned properly.

Murdock slipped an earbud into his ear and performed a communication check with the two men in the back seat.

Soon, Gabbie could see the outermost home marking the edge of the even smaller town of Last Resort, Montana. She slowed as she approached and the speed limit changed.

From what Lyssa had indicated, they would go all the way through Last Resort and out the west end of town. Lyssa hadn't been sure just how far the turn-off for the compound was from Last Resort.

The teen had felt like she'd walked a little more than an hour before she'd come to the edge of Last Resort. Gabbie figured Lyssa had ducked in and out of the shadows, following the highway, which could have slowed her progress. Most likely, the road to the compound was two to three miles outside of Last Resort.

At a mile and a half from town, she slowed. "I don't know if this will be close enough because I'm not exactly sure where the road is, but I don't dare drop you closer and risk a hidden sentry seeing you get out."

"It's all right. This will be close enough," Judge assured her. "And don't stop completely. We'll get out with the truck moving."

Gabbie decreased their speed to a crawl.

Judge and Utah slid out of the back seat and stepped off the running boards like experienced stuntmen. They broke into a jog as soon as their feet hit the ground, disappearing into the shadows beneath the trees.

Gabbie increased her speed only slightly. She didn't want to miss the road to the compound. Turning a horse trailer around never was easy on a narrow highway with skinny shoulders.

She watched as the odometer clicked off tenths of a mile until she'd reached and passed the two-mile mark and still hadn't found the road into the compound.

"There," Murdock pointed ahead to a gap in the trees on the left side of the road.

As Gabbie neared, she could see a well-maintained gravel road leading into the woods.

She cast a glance at Murdock. "Ready?"

His lips twisted. "I should be asking you that same question."

"I'm ready," she said and turned onto the gravel road, easing over the bumps to spare the stallion any undue injury.

She'd only gone twenty yards down the gravel road when two men dressed in black stepped out of the shadows. Each man wielded a military-grade semi-automatic rifle, pointing them at Gabbie and Murdock.

"You are trespassing on private property," said the man on the left. "Turn around and leave, or you will be shot."

"Here goes," Gabbie whispered as she shifted into park.

"Stay in the truck," Murdock said.

"No, I have to do this." She shoved open her door, raised her hands and called out. "Don't shoot! I'm here to deliver a horse to the owner of this property."

Gabbie dropped down from the cab, straightened and stared straight into the barrel of a rifle.

CHAPTER 7

MURDOCK ATTEMPTED to grab Gabbie's arm before she could get out of the truck, but she moved too fast. All he grabbed was air.

Changing direction, he shoved open his door and dropped to the ground, ready to take on anyone who dared lay a hand...or a bullet...on Gabbie.

He hadn't even straightened when the barrel of an AR-15 was shoved into his side.

"Move, and I'll blow a hole straight through you," the man holding the gun warned in a low, guttural tone.

Murdock raised his hands high, his gaze shooting to Gabbie on the other side of the truck, who had the same situation unfolding. He prayed she didn't do anything to anger the man holding the gun to her face. He heard her say she was there to deliver a horse to the property owner.

"You're trespassing," Murdock's gunman accused.

"Sorry, man. We're only here to deliver a horse." He pointed to the horse trailer. "Check him out. He's a beaut."

As if on cue, the stallion whinnied.

"We aren't expecting a horse delivery," the man ground out. "You've got the wrong place."

"Let us talk to the owner," Murdock said. "Maybe he forgot to tell you about his purchase."

"Get back in the truck and leave," his gunman demanded.

"I can't leave until I hand this horse over to its new owner," Gabbie said loud enough for Murdock to hear.

The man holding a gun to Murdock's spleen shoved the barrel into him. "Move."

"Gladly," Murdock said. "You don't have to poke me to get me going." He hurried around the front of the truck to stand beside Gabbie. "Hey, babe. We aren't getting paid enough for this kind of welcome."

Gabbie gave him a tight smile. "We just need to

talk to the owner, hand over the horse and the registration papers and we'll be on our way." She faced the gunman who seemed to be in charge and cocked a pretty, red eyebrow. "Are you going to let us in to see the owner, or do I have to find him myself?"

"You ain't going nowhere," her gunman said through gritted teeth. He pulled a hand-held radio from his pocket and spoke into it. "Got a man and a woman at the entrance saying they have a horse to deliver to the boss." The gunman stared at Gabbie, his weapon's aim never wavering from her face.

Murdock held tightly to his desire to rush the man, take the rifle from his hands and use it to bash his head in. The man even had his finger on the trigger. All he had to do was sneeze, and it would be all over for Gabbie.

"Look, if you let us pass, we'll meet with the owner, give him his horse and we'll be on our way," Murdock said. At the same time, he was assessing his options.

If he wanted, he could easily disarm the two men. But that wasn't their purpose for being there. They needed to get inside the compound and see for themselves how many radicals they'd be up against if Murdock and his team were to stage an extraction.

Most rescues were tricky anyway. But an extraction that involved plucking ten to twenty children from the grasps of volatile survivalists would take a lot of finesse to avoid collateral damage.

As far as Murdock was concerned, not one of those children could end up as collateral damage. They had already endured so much trauma. The kids deserved to be free and happy and back home where they were safe and loved.

His heart hurt for Lyssa and her sister Samantha. They'd been orphaned and landed in the foster care system through no fault of their own. Not all foster families were bad. But losing both parents and being wrenched from the only home they'd known and then placed among strangers must have hit hard.

The hand-held radio the head gunman had in his free hand crackled with static, and a voice said, "Not expecting a horse. Get rid of them."

"Roger," the guard said and slipped the radio back into his pocket. "You heard the boss. You need to leave."

Out of the corner of Murdock's eye, he saw

Gabbie tense. Having already witnessed her obstinance and determination and how the muscles in her face tensed before she went all-in for what she wanted, he could tell she was about to go for it.

Don't do it, Gabbie.

Gabbie planted her fists on her hips and stood toe-to-toe with the man pointing a gun at her head. "Look, I'm just here to deliver a horse. That poor horse has been standing for the last four hours in a tiny space, traveling across bumpy, curvy roads in this godforsaken corner of hell. He needs to be out in a pasture, running, grazing and breathing fresh air, not diesel fumes." She lifted her chin. "Now, if you won't go get your boss, I'll just have to go get him myself."

"Oh, boy," Murdock murmured. "Here we go."

Gabbie spun on her boot heels and marched toward the compound.

"Lady," the leader of the guards shouted. "Stop, or I'll shoot."

"Then I guess you'll have to shoot me," she called out over her shoulder.

"Hey, sweetie," Murdock called out. "Getting shot isn't going to get this horse delivered." He pushed the rifle barrel poking at his spleen to one side and started after Gabbie. "You need to let these nice gentlemen convince their boss to contact the owner about his horse. Taking matters into your own hands isn't going to help." He hurried after her.

"I warned you, lady," the head guard said.

Murdock raced after Gabbie, placing his body between the men holding the guns and the stubborn veterinarian. "Babe, be reasonable."

"I'm tired, I'm hungry and I'm ready to get that horse out of my trailer," she yelled without turning around.

The sharp report of gunfire sounded behind them.

Murdock flung himself at Gabbie, tackling her to the ground.

"I told you to stop," the guard said. "The next bullet won't miss."

Murdock covered Gabbie's body with his and whispered into her ear. "Are you all right?"

"I'm okay," she said. "But that bastard isn't going to be when I get my hands on him."

"He's got the gun," Murdock said. "It might not be a good idea to push him."

"He shot at us," she said.

"My point exactly." Murdock shifted, easing

some of his weight off her. "Promise me you won't attack the man?"

She hesitated. In a tight voice, she said, "I promise."

Murdock pushed to his feet and reached down to give Gabbie a hand.

Once up, she stormed toward the gunman, who was still pointing his weapon at her chest. "Look, mister. I don't know what your problem is, but I have a horse that needs to get out of a trailer. Now, you get your boss to call the owner or—"

The guard leveled his rifle, his eyes narrowing. "Or what?"

"Or nothing," Murdock caught up with Gabbie and slipped his arm around his waist. "We'll just wait patiently for you to contact the owner. No worries."

He planted himself in front of Gabbie and gripped her arms. "Right, babe?"

Red flags of color spotted her cheeks, and fire burned in her eyes. He held her gaze.

Eventually, the spots of color in her cheeks faded, and she gave him a nod.

If he had to, Murdock could take the two guards out. But having Gabbie in the mix would leave her exposed while he took out the guards one at a time. They'd already alerted the compound of Gabbie and Murdock's presence. Any element of surprise was lost. Killing the guards wouldn't buy them anything at that point.

The guards weren't going to let them into the compound. All they could hope for was to drag out their encounter for long enough to allow Drake and Grimm to get into position and observe from a distance. Both men were equipped with binoculars and sights on their rifles. They could zoom in on any movement in and around the compound and report their findings.

Fortunately, they had Lyssa's drawing of the buildings with her understanding of what was inside each. With Drake and Grimm's observations, they could make a plan for the extraction.

For now, they might as well move on and deliver the horse to the appropriate address. Murdock turned toward the truck and trailer.

A movement near the trailer caught his attention, and his pulse leaped.

The guards had their weapons trained on Murdock and Gabbie. Behind them, the side door of the horse trailer opened, and a sandy-blond head poked out. A slim body darted out of the trailer a second later and raced for the tree line.

Lyssa.

The girl hadn't run off after all. She'd managed to stow away inside the trailer. How they'd missed her, Murdock had no idea.

A twig snapped in the woods where Lyssa had disappeared in the shadows.

The guards started to turn toward the sound.

Murdock pulled Gabbie into his arms and whispered urgently into her ear, "Faint, cry, throw a fit or something to get their attention."

Her brow wrinkled. "Why?"

"Just do it," he urged. Murdock shot a glance toward the woods, praying Lyssa would stay down and out of sight. He met Gabbie's gaze. "Now."

She gave him a slight nod. The next moment, her body went limp in his arms, and she sank toward the ground.

Murdock had only a moment to react. He tightened his hold before she could slip through his arms.

Her downward momentum made him stagger and drop to his knees. "Sweet Jesus," he cried.

Immediately, the two guards turned toward him, all attention focused again on Murdock and Gabbie.

"What's her problem now?" the lead guard demanded.

"I'm not sure. All of a sudden, she passed out. She needs a doctor. Is there one here? Or is there somewhere I can lay her down inside a building?"

The guard shook his head. "No strangers are allowed on the premises."

"She could be dying," Murdock cradled Gabbie in his arms. "Do you have a telephone I can use? My cell phone has no reception out here. I need a landline to call for an ambulance."

Again, the guard shook his head. "What part of *you can't stay here*, and *strangers aren't allowed on the premises,* don't you understand?"

"My fiancée needs help," Murdock said, his voice rising. "You have to do something. She might have had a stroke. If she doesn't get to a hospital soon, she could die."

The two guards put their heads together, speaking quietly between themselves. Both frowned and shot irritated glances toward Murdock and Gabbie. After what appeared to be a heated exchange, the head guard pulled the radio out of his pocket and spoke into the mic.

"Sweetheart," Murdock held Gabbie in his arms and stroked her hair back from her forehead.

"Everything is going to be all right." He pressed a kiss to her temple and whispered, "Lyssa."

As soon as the girl's name left Murdock's mouth, Gabbie's eyes popped open. Fortunately, Murdock's body shielded her from the guards' view.

Gabbie closed her eyes again. Barely moving her lips, she whispered, "Where?"

He leaned forward again to press a kiss to her skin just below her ear. "She just came out of the horse trailer," he said so softly the sound wouldn't carry past their ears.

"Holy shit," she murmured under her breath. She moaned softly.

The sound of an engine caught Murdock's attention. He glanced up to see a truck speeding toward them from the compound. It came to a skidding stop, spewing dust, a few feet from where Murdock held Gabbie in his arms.

A tall, barrel-chested man dropped down from the driver's seat. His stubbled chin and the scar stretching from the corner of his right eyebrow to the corner of his lip made him look evil and dangerous.

Murdock wasn't scared. He'd seen worse scars on men he'd fought beside.

The big man's gaze swept over Murdock, Gabbie, the truck and trailer. "What the hell's going on?" he demanded.

Murdock looked up at him from where he knelt on the ground holding Gabbie in his arms. "All we're trying to do is deliver a horse to the owner of this property." He tilted his head. "Is that you?"

"You've got the wrong place. There are no horses here and no place to keep them. Now, get out of here."

Murdock glanced down at Gabbie, who was doing a good job feigning unconsciousness. "We can't leave," he said. "My fiancée passed out. We need to call an ambulance." He held up his cell phone. "And there's no reception here." Murdock met the big guy's gaze. "Do you have a landline at your house that we can call from? These two goons haven't been at all helpful."

Scarface shook his head. "We don't allow strangers on the premises, and we make no exceptions. I suggest you take your woman back into Last Resort and find a phone there."

"Fine. I'll do that. But what about the horse?" he asked. "We get paid for delivering it. If we don't deliver, we don't get paid."

"That's your problem," Scarface said.

Murdock cocked an eyebrow. "Won't your boss be mad when he doesn't get the horse he paid for?" he said, giving it one last shot to get inside the compound.

"My boss didn't order no stinkin' horse, and he doesn't live here. You need to load up and get the hell out of here before we call the sheriff and have you removed or save him the effort and shoot you for trespassing."

Murdock sized up the big man and the two guards. He was sure he could take all three. The frustrated side of him wanted to. These people had stolen children for nefarious reasons. For that alone, he'd take great pleasure in causing them enormous pain while stomping their faces into the ground. However, what would that buy them? It would only alert the rest of the compound to trouble. They'd be on guard.

Lyssa was hellbent on sneaking back in to be with her sister. Chasing after her wasn't an option. She had too much of a lead on him. He'd have to fight his way through the three men before going after the teen.

She'd accomplished what she'd escaped to do.

Her goal had been to seek help to free the children, not just herself.

All he was waiting on now was word from Drake and Grimm. Once they were in position, Murdock and Gabbie would leave.

The small radio earbud crackled in his ear, and Drake's voice sounded, "The eagles have nested."

Thank God. Murdock didn't have to drag out their encounter with the guards and their keeper anymore, waiting for Drake and Grimm to get settled.

Knowing that the two guards and Scarface wouldn't let him and Gabbie into the compound, their best plan of action now was to exit as gracefully as possible.

Murdock gave Scarface a puzzled frown, ready to unentangle them from the guards and leave. "Isn't this where Rayne Williams lives? The GPS led us here with the address he gave us."

"Rayne Williams?" Scarface snorted. "Not hardly. His place is two miles further down the highway."

Murdock stared into the shadows beneath the trees, hoping they'd given Lyssa enough time to return to the compound.

"Are you positive Rayne Williams isn't the

owner of this property and anxiously awaiting the delivery of his horse?" Murdock asked.

"Positive," Scarface said.

"And I can't convince you to let me use a landline to call for an ambulance?" Murdock raised both eyebrows.

"It would be faster to transport her yourself rather than stand here arguing. Absolutely no strangers are allowed on the premises. No exceptions."

Murdock snorted. "So, we've heard. Williams' place is two miles down the road?"

Scarface nodded. "You'll know you're in the right place when you see its massive stone gate. You can't miss it. It's wired with a state-of-the-art security system. You'll have to get permission to pass through the gate."

"Thanks for pointing us in the right direction," Murdock said.

"Just leave and don't come back down this road. The guards are trained to shoot first and ask questions later."

"Why all the security?" Murdock asked. "Is this a celebrity's getaway? Or are you dissecting aliens?" He cocked his eyebrow in challenge.

Scarface's eyes narrowed. "None of your business."

"Message received." Murdock gathered Gabbie in his arms and pushed to his feet.

Gabbie's eyes blinked open, and she stared up into Murdock's face. "What...what happened?"

Murdock smiled down at Gabbie, pleased with how convincing she was about the fainting spell. "You fainted, babe. I knew we should've gotten you something to eat about an hour ago. I'm betting your blood sugar was low."

"I'm okay now," she said. "You can put me down."

"I'm afraid if I do that, you'll pass out again," he said.

Gabbie cupped his cheek and smiled up at him. "You take such good care of me, sweetheart."

He turned his face into her palm and brushed it with his lips. The action felt so natural and right, it shocked him. "You're my one and only."

"If you two are done, could you get a move on?" Scarface grumbled.

Murdock grinned at the man. "She's amazing."

"If I'm amazing, I can stand on my own two feet." She touched his shoulder. "Please, put me down."

Murdock sighed. "As you wish, even though I get great pleasure from holding you this close." Pretending to care about Gabbie was no hardship. He lowered her legs to the ground and steadied her as she got her balance.

"Come on, dear," Gabbie said. "We've taken enough of these men's time, and that horse needs food, water and a chance to stretch his legs."

"Yes, ma'am." Murdock slipped an arm around her waist and led her past the guards to the truck.

When she headed for the driver's side, he shook his head and steered her to the opposite door. "I'll drive. You're not feeling well."

"I'm feeling better already," she insisted but didn't fight him when he opened the passenger door and helped her into her seat.

He closed her door, turned and gave the three men a friendly wave. "Sorry to have bothered you." Murdock slid into the driver's seat and backed the truck and trailer onto the highway, then headed west.

Before they left radio transmission range with the two men left behind, Murdock touched his earbud and said, "Nesting Eagles, Soaring Eagles have left the ground. Solved the mystery, but the

Fledgling got away. Headed your way. Keep it in sight."

"Roger, Nesting Eagle out."

"Soaring Eagle out." Murdock handed Gabbie his cell phone. "Please text Utah and Judge and let them know we found Lyssa. They can head this way. We will need them to execute any plan we come up with."

Gabbie entered the text and sent it, then stared out the window.

"How did we miss her?" she said, her eyes wide and shining with unshed tears. "That poor girl. What will they do to her when she shows up after having disappeared?"

"I don't know." Murdock's stomach roiled at the thought of Lyssa's jailers punishing her for trying to escape. "We need to give Drake and Grimm time to observe. Lyssa's drawing will help, but they know what to look for."

"Can you imagine what would've happened to those kids if we hadn't agreed to deliver a horse?" Gabbie said softly.

"Or stopped at that truck stop when we did, parking in that exact location at that exact time?" Murdock shook his head.

"If I'd gone by myself, I might not have stopped,

preferring to drive straight through," Gabbie snorted softly. "I'm a woman of science. I have to be as a doctor, but I've seen too many miracles not to believe some things were meant to be. Call it fate or whatever you want to call it."

Murdock's lips twisted in a wry grin. "I never considered myself into supernatural phenomenon until I joined the Navy. Since then, I've seen too many unexplainable events to remain too skeptical."

Murdock reached across the console and took her hand. "I believe we have a job to do, and it's not just to deliver a horse."

Gabbie nodded. "We were supposed to be here at this moment in time."

Murdock's fingers tightened around hers. "And we have work to do."

"That's right," Gabbie said. "Those children aren't going to save themselves."

Murdock chuckled. "I don't know. That Lyssa is one very strong-willed young lady. If anyone could organize the children to stage their own coup, Lyssa would be the one."

Gabbie grinned. "Yes, she would." Her brow furrowed. "Slow down. I think we're here."

CHAPTER 8

Murdock shifted his foot from the accelerator to the brake pedal and turned off the highway, bringing the truck and trailer to a halt in front of the massive stone gate Scarface had described.

Beside the gate were a keypad and a camera.

Murdock lowered his window and pressed the button on the keypad.

A voice sounded from an intercom affixed to the keypad. "State your name and purpose."

Murdock's lips twisted. Technology allowed humans to be cold and impersonal.

"Dr. Gabbie Myers and her fiancé, Sean Murdock. Our purpose is to deliver a prize black stallion."

"Proceed," the disembodied voice said.

The wrought iron gate slid sideways.

Murdock drove through the entrance and followed the paved road beneath an arch of over-hanging trees.

The trees' branches grew so closely together they blocked the natural light, giving off the gloomy feeling of dusk.

"It's beautiful." Gabbie shivered. "And creepy."

The road climbed the side of a hill. As they neared the top, the line of trees overhanging the road ended, and the land leveled off in a sprawling plateau with a backdrop of high mountain peaks.

Rising in the middle of the plateau stood a massive, ultra-modern mansion with square corners, two-story windows and views to take your breath away.

"This guy can easily afford a $100,000 horse," Murdock said.

"I wonder how he makes the kind of money that can afford a place like this," Gabbie said.

A young man dressed in black and wearing sunglasses waved at them, directing them to follow him in a tricked-out side-by-side ATV. He led them along a road that swung wide around the house to the stables several hundred yards behind the house. Surrounded by lush green pastures, the stable was as much of an architectural delight as the ultra-modern house.

Murdock pulled in front of the building and shifted into park. The man in black climbed out of the ATV and waited for Murdock and Gabbie to join him at the stable doors.

"Welcome to Cloud Base," the man said. "Please wait here. Mr. Williams will be with you momentarily." He turned and entered the stables, closing the door behind him.

Murdock glanced at Gabbie. "I'm ready to get this done and get the hell out of here."

She nodded. "Me, too. Let's do this."

The door in front of them opened, and a man wearing English riding attire stepped out.

He smiled and strode toward them. "Wonderful. I've been waiting for you to arrive. I thought you'd be earlier." He held out his hand to Gabbie first. "I'm Rayne Williams. You must be Dr. Myers."

She shook his hand. "I am."

"Thank you for taking the time to deliver Lucifer personally. I feel better knowing my horses have the very best of care during transport." He turned to Murdock with one eyebrow cocked.

"Mr. Williams," Gabbie waved a hand toward Murdock. "This is my...fiancé, Sean Murdock. He agreed to come along for the drive to keep me company."

Williams gripped his hand in a firm shake, meeting and holding his gaze. "I'm glad you had company. It's always nice to have backup on any trip."

Murdock shook the man's hand and let go. "Where do you want us to unload your horse? We'd like to get back on the road as soon as possible."

Williams' brow formed a V over his nose. "I had hoped Dr. Myers would stay long enough to ensure Lucifer is settled and not suffering any lasting effects from his move."

"How long were you thinking that I'll need to stay?" Gabbie asked.

Williams' face split in a smile. "I'd hoped you would stay the night. By morning, we can assess the animal. Any issues should be notable by then."

Gabbie's brow puckered. "I didn't come prepared to stay the night. I'd hoped to be back home later this evening."

Williams' smile faded. "We don't have a veterinarian anywhere within a fifty-mile radius. If something were to go wrong with Lucifer in the first twenty-four hours of his arrival, I wouldn't know what to do." He grinned. "Doesn't he come with a warranty? I believe there was wording in the contract to address an overnight stay." He looked from Gabbie to Murdock and back to Gabbie.

Gabbie sighed. "A contract is a contract. We'll find rooms in town, and I can check the stallion now and in the morning before we leave."

"Wonderful." Williams clapped his hands together. "But I would rather you stay with me than in a hotel. I have several guest bedrooms, and my chef is amazing."

Murdock frowned. "That's kind of you, but we don't want to impose."

"You won't be imposing at all. In fact, I insist."

Murdock exchanged a glance with Gabbie.

She shrugged. "I suppose it'll be all right. But we'll have to leave after I check on Lucifer in the morning."

Williams nodded. "Fair enough." He clapped his hands together and glanced toward the horse trailer. "Now, let's get Lucifer settled. Then we can go to the house and have a drink before dinner is served."

Gabbie led the way to the rear of the trailer and released the latches.

ELLE JAMES

Murdock lowered the ramp and stepped inside with Gabbie. Together, they led the stallion down the ramp.

Once off the ramp, Lucifer tossed his head and stamped his hooves.

While Gabbie held the horse's lead, Williams walked all around him. He stopped beside Gabbie, a smile spreading across his face. "He's magnificent," Williams said.

"The Double Diamond is known all over the US and other parts of the world for their excellent horses. I've monitored this stallion's health and growth over the past couple of years. He's perfect."

"Yes, he is," Williams walked up to the stallion and reached out a hand to the animal's nose.

Lucifer tried to rear.

Gabbie held tightly to his halter, keeping him from rising high enough to kick Williams.

The animal dropped down, tossed his head and backed away, whinnying.

Williams frowned. "I take it they haven't worked with him as much as they claimed?"

Gabbie stroked the stallion's nose and spoke softly in soft tones. "They worked with him," she said as if singing a lullaby to Lucifer. "He's just nervous from being in a trailer all day, and now, he's in a strange place."

Murdock was amazed at how quickly she was able to calm the horse.

Gabbie glanced across the horse's nose to Williams. "Where do you want him?"

Williams tipped his head toward the man dressed in black. "My stable hand will take him to the stall we've arranged just for him."

Gabbie gave Williams a tight smile. "If you don't mind, I'd like to get him settled in."

Williams stepped back. "By all means."

Gabbie followed the man in black into the stables.

Murdock started to go in with her.

Williams' voice stopped him. "Did you two get lost trying to find this place?"

Murdock shifted his attention to Williams. "It took us longer than we expected," he answered, choosing vagueness over outright lies.

"We *are* out in the middle of nowhere."

"You have a nice place." Murdock glanced over his shoulder at the mansion behind him. "Why so far out from everything?"

"It suits me," Williams said. "My business takes

me all over the world. It's nice to come home to the peace and solitude of the Rocky Mountains."

Murdock nodded. "Not many people will intrude on your space out here, much less find you."

A smug smile lifted the corners of the other man's mouth. "It's the perfect setup."

"Does it make it more challenging to travel, being so far back in the woods and away from commercial airports?"

Williams shook his head. "Not at all." His lips curled. "It helps to have an airplane parked at the regional airport in Butte."

"That helps." Murdock counted the minutes Gabbie was inside the stables, out of his view, while he was stuck making small talk with the rich man. "What kind of business are you in that takes you all over the world?"

"I design custom security systems for my customers," he said.

"It must be profitable," Murdock nodded toward the stables. "That's not a cheap horse."

"He's not the most expensive horse in my collection. But I liked what I saw and wanted to vary my bloodlines." Williams turned to him. "I have ten horses stabled here. My thoroughbreds are at my farm in Kentucky. Would you like to see the horses I stable here?"

He didn't really want to see the horses as much as he wanted to see Gabbie to make sure she was all right. "Maybe next time."

LEADING LUCIFER, Gabbie had followed the young man dressed in black into the stable. The interior was well-lit, with stalls lining each side. The young man stopped in front of the third stall on the right and opened the gate.

Gabbie walked in with Lucifer. As she passed the young man, she was close enough to notice he wasn't much more than a boy. When he turned to close the gate behind them, his jacket swung open, exposing the handgun tucked into a shoulder holster.

Gabbie's heart fluttered. She could swear the young man wasn't more than fifteen or sixteen. The suit and sunglasses helped make him appear older than he probably was.

On the other side of the stall door, she unclipped the lead from Lucifer's halter.

The stallion went to the water bucket first and drank his fill. Once his thirst was quenched, he explored the bucket of grain and the sections of hay left in a trough.

Gabbie slid a hand down his neck and patted him gently. "You're going to be all right," she said.

She sure hoped he would be. His reaction to Rayne Williams could have been from what she'd said—he was tired, hungry and thirsty and didn't want to be messed with until his basic needs had been fulfilled.

"I can't blame you," she said. After patting his head once more, Gabbie slipped out of the stall and latched it behind her.

The young man stood close by, his hands behind his back, like a soldier at parade rest.

"Do you work with the horses?" Gabbie asked.

"No, ma'am."

"No?" She tilted her head. "Are you part of Mr. Williams' security staff?"

He nodded. "Yes, ma'am."

Her eyes narrowed, but she maintained a smile. "How old are you?"

The boy stiffened and lifted his chin. "Old enough, ma'am."

She glanced into the closest stalls to see other beautiful horses.

"Have you worked for Mr. Williams long?" she

asked without looking in the boy's direction, not wanting to look or sound like she was interrogating him though she was.

He couldn't be old enough to carry a gun. He should be in school like other kids his age, playing football and flirting with girls. What made a boy his age want to work for a billionaire?

Money?

Prestige?

No other choice?

Usually, she'd be curious about the other horses in the billionaire's collection. But, having been with Murdock all day, Gabbie felt a little lost without him at her side.

She emerged from the building alone and joined the two men. "Lucifer seems to have settled down for now. You have some nice horses, Mr. Williams."

He dipped his head. "Thank you, Dr. Myers."

Gabbie didn't insist on the other man calling her by her first name as she did with others. Normally friendly and informal, she wasn't sure why she wasn't with Mr. Williams. Maybe it was the blatant display of his wealth that made her hesitant. Whatever it was, she wasn't changing her mind.

Her gut was telling her to leave as soon as possible. Unfortunately, she couldn't, not when the contract she'd signed included a clause to take the time to ensure the horse settled into his new environment, including an overnight stay.

"If you're hungry," Williams said, "dinner will be served shortly. You should have just enough time to freshen up and change into suitable attire before joining me in the dining room."

"Where should I park my truck and trailer?" Gabbie asked.

Williams waved a hand. "It's fine where it is."

"And as far as changing into more suitable attire," Gabbie glanced down at her jeans and blouse. "What you see is what you get. Like I said, we didn't come prepared to stay a night."

The jeans she slipped on that morning were her best pair. Both the jeans and her blouse were dirty from when Murdock tackled her to keep the TCW guards from putting a bullet through her back. Her heart warmed at the memory of him using his body to shield hers.

"I have something you can wear," Williams said, breaking into her thoughts. "My client in the fashion industry sends me samples of her work for when I have guests who might not have come prepared to stay the night." He dipped his head. "Like yourself. Sometimes, I invite potential clients out to see me. They don't realize how long it takes to get here and get back and end up staying the night." He ran his gaze over Murdock. "My apologies. I don't have formal attire for you. But I have a clean shirt that will fit you."

Murdock nodded.

Gabbie almost laughed at the deadpan expression on Murdock's face. He probably could care less about formal attire. Gabby had never been a girly girl. She could count the times she'd worn a dress on one hand.

She loved what she did for a living, and wearing a dress wasn't required.

Williams led them to the mansion, striding across an impressive patio lined with cushioned lounge chairs and a custom firepit.

He opened a glass door and held it for Gabbie.

When she entered, she stopped and stared for a moment, trying to take it all in.

The two-story ceilings towered above her. One wall was of designer marble with a linear fireplace stretching across it.

Polished marble floors ran the length of the open floor plan. White leather sectional sofas were strategically placed to take advantage of the view through the massive windows.

"If you'll follow my assistant, she will take you to your rooms."

A young woman...no...a girl, probably a teenager, with her hair pulled back in a tight bun at the nape of her neck, stood quietly to one side. She wore a black shirt and trousers, much like the boy in the stables. Without a word, she performed a perfect about-face and walked softly across the marble floor, her shoulders back, her head held high.

She led Gabbie and Murdock up a set of suspended stairs to a second level and turned away from the two-story windows to a bank of doors stretching across the back wall.

At the fourth door to the left, the girl nodded toward Gabbie. "This is your room, ma'am. You'll find everything you might need inside."

"Thank you," Gabbie said but didn't enter.

The girl hesitated as if expecting Gabbie to go in. When Gabbie didn't comply, the girl turned and continued down the row, stopping at the third door from Gabbie's.

"This is your room, sir." The girl took a step back, turned and left him standing there. She walked past Gabbie and disappeared down the staircase.

Murdock backtracked to join Gabbie at her room door. "Let me go in first."

Gabbie nodded and waited outside the door peering in while Murdock made a pass through the room.

He looked under furniture, in closets and even felt around the light fixtures he could reach. When he returned to her, he was frowning.

"What's wrong?" she asked.

"Nothing that I can tell," he said, his voice barely above a whisper.

"But you have a bad feeling about this room?" she said, matching his soft tone.

"About the room, the house, Williams and the kids he's employed."

Gabbie's lips pressed into a tight line. "You noticed that, too? I mean, they could be eighteen."

"But they look younger."

She nodded. "The boy in the stables carried a gun."

Murdock's jaw tightened. "I don't like it, and I don't trust Williams. We should leave."

"With what excuse?" Gabbie said. "My contract

to deliver the horse gives the new owner one night."

"I don't trust him. And I don't trust that the rooms aren't bugged. We have to be careful what we say."

Gabbie reached for Murdock's hand. "One night, and we're out of here."

He squeezed her fingers gently. "Deal."

"Right now, I want to rinse off and dress for dinner. I won't be long."

"Fifteen minutes?" He lifted her hand to his lips and brushed a kiss across the backs of her knuckles.

Her heart fluttered, and warmth spread through her body, pooling low in her belly. "Ten," she breathed.

Murdock backed out of the room and closed the door behind him.

Gabbie fought a rush of panic. She wanted to run after him and beg him to stay with her. It took all her willpower to remain in her room.

Maybe her insecurity had everything to do with their encounter near the compound. She'd never been threatened with being shot before.

Hell, yeah, she was scared. What if those three

survivalists decided she and Murdock were a threat and came looking for them?

For one, they'd have to get past Williams' security system and guards.

With only ten minutes to pull herself together, Gabbie hurried through the room and entered the connecting bathroom. She stripped and stepped into the shower, rinsing off the dirt and the smell of horse. She didn't wash her hair, knowing it would take thirty minutes to dry.

Gabbie dried off her body, wrapped the towel around herself and stepped out into the bedroom. The closet door stood open with several items hanging inside.

Curious about Williams' clothes designer client, she crossed to the closet and studied the selection.

Three dresses hung on satin hangers, wrinkle-free and absolutely stunning. Any one of them could be worn to a red-carpet event in Los Angeles. In the backwoods of Montana, they were overkill.

The fourth dress could be worn on the red carpet, but it wasn't as over-the-top elaborate as the other three. A simple black dress of silky material, it was understated and lovely.

Gabbie pulled it off the hanger and slipped it over her head. The fabric slid over her body, feather-soft and light, the hem falling to mid-calf. The back of the dress dropped all the way down to the small of her back.

The dress fit like a second skin, hugging every curve of her body.

Gabbie stared at her reflection in the full-length mirror and wondered what Murdock would think of her in the dress. Her pulse quickened. All it would take would be to slip the thin straps over her shoulders, and the dress would fall to the floor.

Heat rushed into her cheeks and throughout her body. She'd never felt this passionate about any man. Until Murdock.

The dress was amazing. But what about shoes?

She returned to the closet and found several boxes of shoes. One of the boxes had a pair of shiny silver, strappy sandals that would complement the dress. She pulled them out of the box and slipped her feet onto them. They were a little big, but she tightened the strap to make them work.

With only two minutes left of her ten, she ran back to the bathroom, grabbed a brush and dragged it through her crazy red hair. She didn't have time to do much with it, so she pulled it up on top of her head and secured it in a messy bun, allowing a few tendrils to frame her face.

She dug through the drawer in the bathroom and found some makeup. Not ever good at contouring or making smoky eyes, she brushed a little blush on her cheeks, applied some mascara and sighed.

Her time was up, and she was as good as she would get. She wished she had paid more attention to the other girls in high school and college who were so good at dressing up and applying makeup.

A soft knock on her door sent her running across the room, her pulse racing.

She flung open the door and stared up at Murdock, her mouth going dry at how very handsome he was. He'd showered, shaved and combed his dark wet hair back from his forehead.

The crisp white button-down shirt Williams had provided emphasized the darkness of his hair and the ice blue of his eyes.

The man made Gabbie absolutely weak at the knees.

"Wow," he said.

"Wow, yourself," she said, her voice breathy like

she couldn't get enough air into her lungs to speak properly.

He took her hands, his gaze going from the top of her head to the tips of her toes in the strappy sandals. "You are stunning."

Heat rose from her chest into her cheeks and spread throughout her body. "Thank you."

"It's too bad we have to go down to dinner with Williams."

She nodded, thinking of other things they could be doing instead. If her cheeks could have gotten any hotter, they would have. Gabbie was heading into dangerous territory that would end in heartbreak. Murdock was her protector. Not her date. Not her real fiancé. Not anyone with any obligation to love her.

Was she willing to risk her heart with a man who would likely walk away at the end of his assignment?

For one night with this man, would it be worth it?

Her logical brain tried to tell her no while her heart screamed, *Yes*!

"Shall we join our host for dinner?" he asked.

His words broke through her wild fantasies of

pulling him into her room, closing the door and making love with him through the night.

Gabbie sighed. "I guess so."

Murdock chuckled. "I feel the same. But we can't stand him up, can we?"

She met his gaze for a long moment. Finally, she shook her head. "No."

Murdock held out his arm.

Gabbie slipped her hand through the crook of his elbow and walked down the stairs with him.

The girl who'd led them to their rooms stood at the bottom of the stairs. As soon as they reached the ground level, she said, "Please, follow me." She turned and led the way across the opulent living room. The sun had disappeared behind the mountain peaks, and darkness had settled in. Subtle lighting throughout the room made it easy for them to navigate while allowing them to take in the view outside the window as stars appeared in the night sky.

Williams' assistant led them into a dining room with three charcoal-gray walls and a wall of windows. A glass dining table that could seat twelve guests occupied the center of the room with a modern LED chandelier that resembled the infinity symbol. One end of the table had been set with clear crystal glasses, silver charger plates and black dishes.

Rayne Williams stood at the window, dressed in a black suit. He turned when they entered the room and smiled. "Oh, good. The chef just informed me that dinner is ready to be served. Please, take a seat."

Williams held out the seat next to him for Gabbie. "Dr. Myers, you look lovely this evening.

"Thank you," she said as she sank onto the black velvet seat.

Murdock took the seat next to hers.

William nodded to his assistant, who left the room and returned moments later carrying a bottle of wine.

She was followed by three other young women, carrying the first course, a salad of spinach, chunks of apple and dried cranberries topped by a light vinaigrette.

One course followed another, each better than the last—all worthy of the finest restaurants in the country.

The conversation was limited to discussing nearby national parks, the plight of the wolves that had been reintroduced to Yellowstone and the weather.

Gabby counted the minutes until the dinner was over, wanting to return to her room. In her head, she rehearsed what she would say to Murdock to get him to stay with her rather than sleep in the room he was assigned.

As the staff cleared the last plate from the table and coffee was served, Williams' assistant entered, crossed to him and bent to whisper something in his ear.

He frowned and whispered something back.

The girl left the room.

"Please excuse me. I have a matter I must deal with. I won't be long. My chef has dessert prepared if you've saved room."

Without waiting for any response, he rose from the table and left the dining room.

Murdock pushed back from the table, stretched and moved to the window.

Gabbie joined him. "Are you as ready as I am to call it a night?"

He slipped his arm around her and pulled her close. "Past ready."

Movement on a patio below them caught Gabbie's attention. "Isn't that our host?"

Murdock nodded. "Looks like it, but who is that with him?"

Williams' body blocked their view of the other man. Whatever they were discussing had Williams tense. He turned and walked away a few steps, then spun and faced the man, still talking.

One of the patio lights shone down onto the other man's face. Even from a distance, Gabbie could see the jagged scar from the corner of his eyebrow to the corner of his mouth.

Gabbie gasped.

CHAPTER 9

MURDOCK UTTERED A CURSE. "What's *he* doing here?"

Williams spoke again.

The man nodded, turned and left.

Their host stood for a long moment, watching the man as he walked away. Then he turned toward the house.

Murdock quickly pulled Gabbie away from the window. They returned to their seats and lifted their coffee cups.

"The almanac indicates we'll have a hard winter," Gabbie said as Williams reentered the dining room and took his seat.

"Does that mean you'll be busier than normal?" Murdock asked.

"Probably," Gabbie smiled at Williams. "Do you follow the Farmer's Almanac?"

Williams shook his head. "I don't. Do its predictions really come true?"

Gabbie shrugged. "Sometimes. About as often as the weathermen get it right."

Murdock set his coffee cup on the table. "If you don't mind, we'd like to call it a night."

"Yes. It's been a long day," Gabbie said, "and we'll be rising early in the morning to check on Lucifer before we hit the road home."

"Certainly. I completely understand. I'm sorry I had to leave the table. One of my neighbors stopped by for a moment."

"Everything all right?" Murdock asked.

Williams nodded. "Absolutely." He rose from the table and held Gabbie's chair as she stood.

"Thank you for an extraordinary dinner," Gabbie said. "And for the use of this amazing dress."

"Yes, yes. I'm glad you enjoyed it." He nodded toward the girl standing near the door. "If you need help finding your room, my assistant will show you the way. I hope you sleep well. Good night."

Williams turned and left the room.

Murdock reached for Gabbie's hand. "We can find our way to our rooms," he said to the girl standing quietly against the wall.

She nodded and left the room.

Gabbie exchanged a look with Murdock.

He gave her a quick nod, and they left the dining room, passed through the living room and climbed the stairs.

Murdock entered Gabbie's room, making a quick pass-through before he allowed her inside.

Once Gabbie entered, she quickly closed the door behind her, trapping him inside. "Please stay."

He stared down into her eyes. "Are you sure?"

"Positive. I don't trust—"

Murdock touched his finger to her lips and shook his head.

Her eyes widening, she nodded.

Then Murdock bent and brushed his lips across hers and whispered. "Come with me."

He led her into the adjoining bathroom and turned on the shower.

With the sound of the water filling the room, he pulled her into his arms. "I don't know why that man was here, but I think we need to leave."

She looked up at him, her brow furrowing. "Now?"

Murdock shook his head. "No. We need to wait until everyone is bedded down for the night and then slip out. The truck will make noise, but that can't be helped. Hopefully, by the time they realize we're leaving, we'll be well on our way."

"I don't know. He's got a robust security system. I don't think we'll get far before they're onto us. Stay here. I want to check something."

He left her in the bathroom and crossed to the bedroom door.

Gabbie watched from the bathroom door, the shower still running behind her.

Murdock opened the bedroom door and left her room, closing the door behind him.

Gabbie's breath caught and held. After a full minute, she couldn't stay put a moment longer. She crossed the bedroom and reached for the doorknob.

When it turned in her hand, she released it and jumped back.

Murdock pushed it open. He glanced over his shoulder, waved and called out, "Good night." He entered her room, carrying the shirt he'd arrived in, and quickly closed the door behind him.

Once again, Murdock pulled her into the bathroom with the shower running and spoke softly, "I went to the room they assigned me to collect my shirt. There's a man standing at the top of the staircase. He's armed."

Gabbie's heart pounded against her ribs.

Murdock turned off the bedroom light, crossed the room to the window and pushed the curtain aside.

Gabbie stood beside him and peered out.

Murdock whispered close to her ear. "There's a guard at each corner of the house. You can see them just past the glow of the security lights."

Gabbie stared out into the darkness. She couldn't see anyone. Then a shadow shifted, and she could make out a figure standing at the corner of the house and another on the other corner.

"What should we do?" she murmured, her heart beating so fast she felt lightheaded.

Murdock stood for a long moment, staring out at the night. "Like you suggested…we wait. Let them think we're going to sleep. Maybe they'd relax their vigil, and we can sneak past them."

"You don't really think they'll be that easy to get past, do you?" she said softly.

"Not really, and I'm thinking we might have to leave the truck and trailer behind and just get out."

Gabbie had been afraid of that. "My truck is my

livelihood," she murmured, then squared her shoulders. "But our lives are more important."

Murdock pulled her into his arms and held her. "Are you up for this?"

She nodded. "We have to get out of here. Lyssa and Samantha need us."

"All the children need us." Murdock pulled his cell phone from his pocket and stared at the screen. "No reception and I haven't heard the guys over the radio."

"When do you want us to make our move?" Gabbie asked.

"Let's aim for one AM. Hopefully, the guards will get lax by then, and we can sneak out without them knowing."

"If we can make it to the trees, we'll at least be able to hide." Gabbie frowned, remembering the huge stone gate at the entrance to Williams' estate. "Is this entire estate fenced?"

"My bet is yes."

"How will we get over it?" she asked.

"We'll cross that bridge when we come to it." He brushed a strand of her hair away from her face. "First, we have to get away from the mansion."

"We have four hours to kill before that," she reminded him.

"We should get some rest."

She laughed. "That's not going to happen."

"You can sleep. I'll keep watch," he said.

Gabbie shook her head. "I'm so wound up I couldn't begin to close my eyes."

"You'll be exhausted before we even begin." He led her to the bed. "At least lie down and put your feet up."

"Only if you rest as well," she said.

"Deal." Murdock glanced down at her dress. "By the way, you look amazing in that dress and those shoes."

"Thank you." Her cheeks heated as she remembered what she'd fantasized about earlier. Now that they were considering escaping the mansion, making love was probably the last thing he'd want to do.

His finger traced the strap across her shoulder. "You know, as amazing as you are in that dress, I like the Gabbie I first met, wearing jeans and boots and riding like a badass to my rescue. When your hat blew off and your hair flew out behind you, I was hooked."

She snorted. "You were too busy holding on for dear life to even notice me."

He raised his hand to the tendril of red hair curling around her chin. "I noticed, in between fearing for my life. Red hair is hard to miss."

She reached up and pulled the elastic band holding her messy bun in place. Her hair fell around her shoulders, thick and wavy. "Red hair is the bane of my existence."

"No way. It's what makes you special. That and the way you care for animals and people." He twisted a finger into one of her curls. "I like your red hair." He cupped her cheek and brushed his thumb across her lips. "I like so much about you."

Gabbie's pulse quickened and swirled at her core. She stared up into his face. The starlight shining through the window gave him a blue glow. She leaned her face into his palm and pressed her lips to his skin. "I've never been good at relationships. I don't know how to flirt or how to seduce someone I don't know or how to read into words or expressions, and I've never had an orgasm. Or at least I don't think I have." She covered his hand on her face and met his gaze.

Murdock chuckled. "Never had an orgasm?" He

shook his head. "Sweetheart, you don't know what you've been missing."

"Exactly. And what I'm beating around the bush about is—" Gabbie drew in a deep breath and spat it out, "I want to make love with you. When I'm near you, I get hot all over and want to get naked with you." She laughed. "I've never felt like that before, so I have to conclude that I'm sexually attracted to you."

"Is that a scientific conclusion? Or are you throwing science to the wind to embrace the possibility of fate playing its hand?"

"Both." Gabbie closed her eyes and braced herself for rejection. "Look, I understand that just because I'm attracted to you doesn't mean you're attracted to me. Although, you did say you liked me. Or at least that you liked me better in jeans and boots."

She threw her hands in the air. "Hell, I'm botching this, aren't I? Bottom line is, I want you. If you don't feel the same, I'll understand, and I won't bring it up ever again." She rested a hand on his chest and stared at where her fingers curled into the borrowed shirt. "But if you feel even a little of the same desire and want to make love, I'm all in."

When Murdock didn't answer immediately, Gabbie dared to look up into his eyes.

His lips curled in a gentle smile.

"Oh, hell. You're not interested." Gabbie started to back away.

His arm circled her waist, and he pulled her to him. "You've got that wrong. I'm stunned that you think I'm not interested. Did you hear the words I said?"

Gabbie nodded slowly and then shook her head.

"I said I liked your red hair. I said I liked so much about you. I was hooked when you came to my rescue."

"Liked? What does that mean? I told you I'm not good at reading cues. Does that mean you like me like a kid sister? Or do you like me like someone you want to make love to?"

He cupped her cheeks in his palms and tipped her head up. "I want to make love with you, Gabbie Myers. I want to be the one who gives you your first orgasm. And believe me, you'll know it's an orgasm when it's for real."

She drew in a deep breath and let it out in a whoosh. "Whew! That's a relief. For a moment there, I thought I'd just made the biggest fool of myself, and I would never be able to look you in the eye ag—"

Murdock cut off her words with a crushing kiss that stole her breath away and scrambled her thoughts. She leaned into him, rising on her toes to deepen the kiss. When he swept his tongue across her lips, she opened to him.

His hands slid down her back and lowered to rest on her hips, bringing her close enough to feel the evidence of his desire pressing into her belly.

Heat seared through her veins, bringing out the wanton in her she never knew existed. Gabbie leaned back and worked loose the buttons on his shirt. One by one, she freed them, pulling the shirttail from his waistband to finish the task. Then she pushed the shirt over his broad shoulders and down his muscular arms, her hands smoothing over his taut skin as she reveled in his strength.

He shifted his weight and toed off first one boot and then the other.

Gabbie reached for his belt, unbuckled it and pulled it free of the belt loops, letting it drop to the floor. Then she pushed the button free on the waistband of his jeans and slid the zipper downward.

His cock sprang free, jutting out, hard and straight.

Fascinated by how long and thick it was, she wrapped her hands around it. It was as hard and soft like stone encased in velvet. She ran her fingers along its length, stroking and touching, getting to know the smooth ridges.

Murdock captured her hand and held it still. "You know, you're killing me, don't you?"

She frowned up at him. "Does that hurt when I touch you there?"

"Only in the best way." He raised her hand to his lips and pressed a kiss to her palm. "But I won't last long if you keep that up. And I want to get you there first."

"Oh." She drew in a ragged breath and let it out slowly. "Would it help if I was naked?" She raised her hand and slipped the thin strap of her dress over her shoulder.

Murdock caught her before she slipped the other one free. "Let me," he said and kissed her mouth in a long, sensual coupling of their tongues that left her knees weak and desire burning at her core.

Abandoning her mouth, he blazed a path of kisses down the length of her neck, pausing at the base of her throat where her pulse beat wildly. Then he kissed his way across her shoulder to the remaining strap, sliding it slowly over the edge.

As she'd imagined, the dress slithered over her breasts, down her torso and past her hips, falling in a pool of fabric around her ankles.

Gabbie stepped free and started to bend to remove the strappy sandals from her feet.

Murdock stopped her by catching her hand and raising it to his lips. "Not yet. There's something incredibly sexy about a woman in heels and nothing else."

Her pulse spiked at the intensity of his gaze as he stepped back and looked at her from the tips of her breasts to her toes.

Had he looked at her any other way, she might have felt compelled to cover herself.

But the way his gaze caressed her made her feel...beautiful.

Murdock slid his hands over her shoulders and down her arms to her hips. He reversed the direction, following the curve of her waist up to the swell of her breasts. Cupping them in his palms, he squeezed gently and then tweaked the nipples between his thumbs and forefingers.

He bent to take one nipple into his mouth and

flicked his tongue across the tip until it hardened into a little bead.

Gabbie laced her fingers in his hair and held him to her breast, her hips rocking slightly with each flick or nip.

She ached for more, wanting him inside her.

Murdock hooked his thumbs in the elastic waistband of her panties and slid them over her hips and downward, his hands caressing her hips, her thighs, her calves all the way down to her ankles.

He knelt in front of her and lifted one foot at a time to remove the undergarment, pressing a kiss to her calves on his way back up. He guided her backward until she bumped into the bed and sat on the edge.

Murdock placed his hands on her knees and spread her legs, his fingers sliding along her inner thighs, his mouth following with flicks of his tongue.

As he neared her center, her breath lodged in her throat, and her pulse pounded through her veins.

When his fingers touched her there, Gabbie moaned.

He parted her folds with his thumbs and

stroked that nubbin of flesh, igniting her firestorm of desire into a raging inferno.

When his mouth closed on that same nubbin, he flicked it with his tongue. The first time was deliciously shocking. The second flick made her fingers and toes curl. The third jettisoned her into an explosion of sensations so intense she forgot to breathe, so focused was she on riding that feeling to the very last electric current tingling from her core to the very tips of her fingers and toes.

She fell back against the mattress, dragging air back into her lungs. "Oh, sweet Jesus," she gasped. "You were right. Oh, so right."

He chuckled, his breath warm against her sex. "Now, you know what you've been missing."

"Yes. I. Do." She reached for him. "But it's not enough."

He laughed. "Getting greedy? Wanna go for round two?"

"I ache for more," she said. "I want you. Inside me." She sat up and wrapped her arms around his neck. "Please."

With her still holding on around his neck, he rose, swinging her up in his arms. He kissed her as he laid her on the bed, then stepped back.

He fished his wallet out of his back pocket and

plucked a packet from inside. Then he shed his jeans and kicked them to the side.

He stood for a moment, starlight bathing his muscular body in an indigo-blue glow. His cock stood straight and thick.

He was magnificent.

"If at any time this isn't right for you, just tell me, and I'll stop," he said.

"Shut up and come to me," she said, her voice choked with her desire.

He climbed onto the bed and leaned over to kiss her lips.

She parted her legs, and he settled between them, the tip of his cock, nudging her entrance.

Murdock rose to his knees and ripped open the packet.

Gabbie took the condom from him and rolled it over his engorged staff, loving that she'd made him that hard and that she'd soon have him inside her.

She lay back against the pillow, gripped his hips and guided him into her slick channel.

He moved slowly, filling her, stretching her to fit his length and girth. Once he'd sunk all the way to the hilt, he pulled almost all the way out.

Impatient for more, Gabbie gripped his hips

and brought him home again. She set the pace, increasing the speed until Murdock took control, pumping in and out, faster and harder.

Gabbie raised her knees and planted her heels in the mattress, rising to meet him at every thrust.

Murdock's body tensed, and he thrust once more, driving deep into her. He stayed buried, his cock pulsing inside her.

Gabbie wrapped her legs around Murdock, holding him close until he finally collapsed against her, his body crushing the air from her lungs.

He only lay there for a moment before he rolled onto his side, taking her with him.

"I'm glad you were my first," she whispered and laughed. "My first orgasm. Thank you for making it memorable."

He laughed. "I don't think anyone has ever thanked me for making love to her."

"Well, they should have." Gabbie moved closer, resting her cheek against his broad chest. "Just so you know, I don't expect anything from you. No strings, no commitment." She rested her hand on his chest, wishing they could stay like they were at that moment, forever. "We're two consenting adults. I promise not to make any crazy demands."

"Oh, yeah?" Murdock rose on one elbow and

stared down at her face in the limited light from the stars. "What if I want strings or I crave commitment?"

She cupped his cheek. "It's too soon. We barely know each other. Until we do, we shouldn't make any rash promises in the heat of passion that we might regret later." She gave him a tight smile.

He frowned. "Is this your way of giving me the brush-off and making it sound like you're doing me a favor?"

"No, that's not what this is."

"Don't you believe in fate and love at first sight?"

She grimaced. "I told you. I believe some things were meant to be. But the scientist in me wants to prove the theory before I make my conclusions."

"And I believe life is short, and you have to go for the joy whenever and wherever you find it." He leaned down and pressed his lips to hers. "For some strange reason, I can't explain...you bring me joy." He held up his hands. "Don't worry, I won't campaign for commitment or promises, even though I believe fate brought us together when my horse ran away with me. And I won't speak of undying love until you've had time to prove your theory."

"Thank you," she said.

Murdock shook his head. "My gut tells me to hold onto you and never let go. So, I'll give you the time you need, but I'm not going anywhere. I'll be here when you come to your conclusion. One that I already know. We were meant to be."

CHAPTER 10

GABBIE HAD FALLEN ASLEEP. She woke when Murdock shook her several times.

He hated waking her, but they needed to get moving

"What?" Gabbie said, sitting up straight and blinking.

Murdock leaned over and kissed her. "Wake up. It's time to go."

It took a moment or two for her sleep-fogged brain to engage. When it did, she swung her legs over the side of the bed and pushed to her feet. "I'm ready."

Murdock chuckled as he slipped his radio earbud in his ear. "You might want to put on some clothes. It gets cold at night in the mountains."

"Right." Gabbie gathered her jeans and shirt and walked across the room to the bathroom.

"Have I told you how sexy you are naked?" Murdock said as she passed by him.

"No, but feel free to knock yourself out." She winked as she went by and stepped into the bathroom.

Minutes later, she was dressed and combed, and her hair was pulled back in a neat ponytail at the back of her head. She emerged from the bathroom wearing her own clothes, with no makeup and looking a little ragged around the edges with less than two hours of sleep.

She was still the woman he admired most. Hers was the last face he wanted to see at night and the first one he wanted to see in the morning.

Had they only known each other for two days?

"I'm going to leave the room first," Murdock said as he stood near the bedroom door. "If the guard tries to stop me, I'll have to deal with him. I'd prefer if you'd give me a couple of seconds before you come out."

Gabbie leaned up on her toes and kissed him. "Be careful. I want to keep you around a little longer."

Though she smiled, it was tight, and the light didn't shine from her eyes.

He gave her a quick kiss and opened the door. After a quick look, he ducked out and pulled the door closed behind him.

The hallway was mostly dark, with nightlights placed to mark a path for its length.

Murdock moved silently to the top of the stairs where he'd last seen the armed guard. He was nowhere to be seen.

He didn't trust that leaving Williams' mansion would be easy. The guards were there. He just hadn't run across them yet.

Back at the room he'd shared with Gabbie, he opened the door. "Let's go."

She slipped through the door and walked with him to the top of the staircase.

With Murdock in the lead, they descended the stairs to the main level and hurried across the living area to the door they'd come through the day before.

"Be ready. I'm not sure what will happen if we're discovered. It would be best if neither of those scenarios came to pass. But if they do...run."

Murdock pushed the door open.

Immediately, a siren wailed, and lights blinked.

"Now would be a good time to run!" Murdock grabbed her hand and ran to the end of the patio and down the steps to the ground below.

Guards came from both sides, carrying military-grade semi-automatic rifles.

"Halt, or we'll shoot!" one guard cried.

With guards on either flank, Murdock and Gabbie ran straight, heading toward the stables.

"Halt!" the voice called out again.

With little cover available between the house and the stables, they were exposed and could be easily picked off if the man with the rifle was a decent shot.

Once committed to this course of action, they couldn't stop.

Murdock insisted Gabbie run ahead of him. Thankfully, she was in good shape and a fast runner.

By the time they reached the horse trailer, they'd managed to put a little distance between themselves and their pursuers. Not much, maybe a few seconds. Knowing they didn't have much time, Murdock ran straight for the horse trailer, quickly dropped the ramp and dove inside with Gabbie.

He shoved aside the divider walls until he reached the last one. Murdock almost whooped for joy at the sight of his motorcycle. He'd almost expected it to be gone.

He leaped onto the seat and leaned forward to make room for Gabbie.

As she slid onto the back, Murdock turned the key and started the engine. It immediately roared to life.

"Hold on!" Murdock twisted the throttle as Gabbie's arms tightened around his middle.

The bike shot out of the back of the trailer and raced away from the stables.

Shots rang out behind them.

Gabbie hugged him tighter.

He hated that she was on the back. If the gunmen were lucky enough to hit the pair on the motorcycle, Gabbie would be the one to take the bullet.

All the more reason to get out of range as soon as possible.

Murdock sped along the road leading to the gate. If it didn't open automatically, they'd just have to find another way out, even if it meant ditching the bike and climbing over the wall.

They reached the wall well ahead of the two guards who had been on foot.

The gate did not open automatically.

Quickly ditching the bike, Murdock and Gabbie ran along the gate wall until they found where the stone wall ended, and the six-foot-tall perimeter fence stretched into the distance.

"You go first." Murdock bent, laced his hands together, and said, "Step into my hands and jump for the top. I'll help you get there.

Gabbie placed her boot in Murdock's hands. As he rose, she flung herself over the top of the wall and dropped down to the other side.

She looked up, waiting for Murdock to join her.

"Come on, Sean!"

Intent on watching for Murdock, she didn't realize she wasn't alone until a hand clamped over her mouth and nose. Something sickly sweet filled her nostrils.

Gabbie fought to get free until a black abyss consumed her.

AFTER HELPING Gabbie over the wall, Murdock backed up for a running start. Just as he was about to take off, he was hit from the side and knocked to the ground. Someone landed on top of him.

Survival instinct set in. Murdock bucked and

rolled in an attempt to get out from under the man holding him down. He felt a sharp stick in the back of his neck and a burning sensation. When he finally managed to slip out from beneath the big man, he rolled to his feet, staggered a few steps and fell to his knees.

Gabbie. Must get to Gabbie.

His vision blurred. He shook his head in an attempt to clear the fog, but everything faded to black.

WHEN GABBIE CAME TO, she blinked in an attempt to open her eyes, only to realize they were open, but she was in a place so dark not a fraction of light came through. She couldn't move her arms. They were secured behind her back with something hard and plastic. As the brain fog cleared bit by bit, she remembered being caught from behind and a hand with a cloth pressing over her mouth and nose.

Zip ties.

Her wrists and ankles had been bound with zip ties.

Murdock.

Her heart pounded in her chest.

"Murdock," she called out. "Murdock!"

Something stirred in the darkness.

Her mind went crazy with images of rats gnawing at her skin.

"Murdock," she called out. "You'd better be here with me. Damn it, Murdock! We've come too far together. Answer me!"

A low groan sounded from several feet away.

"Is that you, babe?" she asked, a sob rising in her throat. "Please talk to me and prove you're not a rat."

Gabbie listened, praying for a miracle.

Another groan sounded.

"Wake up, Murdock. Sean. Sweetie." Tears trickled down her cheeks. "You have to wake up. That part about how we were meant to be is true. I was too scared to believe it. I told you, I'm no good at relationships. But I can learn. I want to learn with you. Murdock, wake up!"

"Awake," said a gravelly voice barely better than a croak.

"Murdock? Is that really you?" Her tears flowed faster. "You're alive?" Gabbie struggled to a sitting position and then scooted on her butt toward the location she'd heard his voice.

She'd gone several feet when she bumped into

something on the floor.

"Hey, sweetie, is that you?" With her hands behind her back, she couldn't reach out and feel for him. Instead, she leaned over and fell on top of the lump.

It moved and croaked. "Gabbie."

"Yes," she said, her heart leaping. "Murdock, wake up. We have to get out of here."

"Zip-tied," he whispered.

"Yeah. Me too. And it's so dark." Despite the darkness, Gabbie dared to hope. She was with Murdock. Together, they'd figure out a way to break their bonds and escape.

"I'm glad you're alive," she said.

"Same." He shifted beneath her.

Gabbie pushed to a sitting position. "Are your hands tied behind your back as well?"

"Yes."

"Are you able to sit up?"

"I think so." After a bit of rustling and a couple of curses, Murdock said, "I'm up. My head is spinning, but I'm sitting up."

"Good, I'm going to scoot around the floor and see if I can find something sharp to rub against the zip ties." Inch by inch, Gabbie scooted around the floor, feeling behind her for jagged metal, broken glass, or anything she could use to sever the ties. The floor and walls of the room they were in were smooth and free of debris.

"No luck?" he asked.

She sighed. "None."

"Come closer."

Gabbie scooted back to where she'd found Murdock and leaned against him. "Are you feeling all right?"

"Better every minute. Stay still." Murdock tipped onto his side and lay on the ground behind her. "Hold out your arms. I'm going to bite through the zip tie."

Gabbie held out her arms.

Murdock moved closer and nuzzled her wrists until he bit down on the plastic restraint with his teeth. After sawing and biting on it for several minutes, the plastic broke.

Gabbie pulled her wrists apart and rubbed where the tie had scraped her skin. "Thank you. Now to free you." She waited for him to sit up again, then lay down and chewed at the zip tie on Murdock's wrists until it broke.

Without a knife, they had to repeat the process two more times until their ankles were free.

Murdock stood and helped Gabbie to her feet.

They felt the walls around their prison and didn't find a door or window.

"Feels like the walls are hard-packed dirt," Gabbie said. "Could we be in a cave, basement or bunker?"

"Could be one of them. The door has to be above us." Murdock touched her arm. "I can lift you while you feel for a trap door. I'm bending down. Climb onto my shoulders, and I'll stand.

"Are you steady enough after what they gave you?"

"I am." He knelt.

Gabbie sat on his shoulders and held on as he rose to his feet.

He moved around the room while Gabbie felt above their heads for a door.

"The ceiling is wood with joists holding them up." She moved to the left and pushed against the wood. It didn't budge.

Murdock moved to the left, one step. Gabbie pushed against the ceiling. This time, the wood lifted.

"This has to be it." She pushed again, and the door lifted three inches.

"Can you see anything?" Murdock asked.

She pushed again and tried to see what was on

the other side of the wooden ceiling. "It's dark up there too, but there might be some moonlight shining through a window somewhere. I think I see table legs."

Murdock squeezed Gabbie's legs. "Shhh."

Gabbie lowered it carefully and listened to what sounded like footsteps in the room above.

"Get it done. We're moving out in five minutes," a voice called out from a distance.

"I'll be done," a gravelly voice responded from somewhere directly above Murdock and Gabbie.

Sounds of splashing liquid were quickly followed by an acrid scent that stung Gabbie's nose. Her heart plunged to the pit of her belly. "He's pouring gasoline up there."

A moment later, fire lit the room above, the glow bright enough to illuminate the cellar below.

"We have to get out," Murdock said. "Now. You have to throw open that trap door."

Gabbie shoved as hard as she could. The door rose a foot and slammed back down. Again, she tried to throw the door back, only managing to open it a foot. Flames burned through the gasoline and lit walls of the room above them.

"I'm not strong enough to open that door," Gabbie cried. "Let me down."

Murdock released her legs, and she slid down his back, landing hard on the dirt floor, staggering backward before she righted herself and dropped to her hands and knees. "Get on my back," she yelled.

Murdock shook his head. "I weigh too much."

"I can do this, and you have to open that door. Do it! We don't have much time."

Murdock eased onto her back and raised his hands over his head. His first attempt ended much like Gabbie's. The second push sent the trap door higher.

"Come on, Murdock. Three's a charm," she called out, the pressure on her back not nearly as painful as the thought of being burned alive.

Murdock gave a mighty heave that strained Gabbie's back.

She held her breath and waited for the door to clang back down quickly. A second passed, then another, and finally, a different clanging sounded.

"It's open," Murdock announced. "I'm going up."

A moment later, the weight on Gabbie's back disappeared. She staggered her feet and coughed as smoke infiltrated the cellar.

For a frightening few seconds, she couldn't see

Murdock. Then he dropped down on his stomach at the edge of the trap door and reached down to Gabbie. "Grab my hand," he said.

She stood on her toes and stretched as high as she could but came up three inches short of Murdock's fingertips.

Smoke roiled to the ceiling in the room above as fire ate into the walls and floor.

"Jump up," Murdock cried. "You can do it."

Gabbie jumped. Her fingers touched Murdock's, but she couldn't get a grip on his hand. Flames rose all around him.

"Get out," she cried. "You have to get out."

"Jump! I'll catch you."

"Leave me and save yourself," she said. "Go!"

"I'm not leaving without you. We're meant to be together. Alive. Not dead. Now jump like your life depends on it." He reached down as far as he could.

Gabbie backed up a few steps and went for a running jump, reaching as high as her arm could stretch.

Murdock caught her hand in a wrist lock.

He had leaned so far down her weight threatened to take them both down into the cellar.

Murdock held on, waited until he'd regained

his balance and then inched away from the edge. Once he stabilized, he reached down with his other hand and pulled her up to the ledge. "Hold on to the edge for a moment. I have to let go so I can get a lower grip to pull you the rest of the way up."

"I'll try." She shifted her grip from his hands to the rigid steel frame. As soon as she released Murdock's hand, she gripped the edge. Immediately, her fingers slid. "I can't hold on," she said.

"Don't worry," Murdock said. "I've got you."

He leaned over the opening to the cellar, grabbed Gabbie's belt loops and rolled her over the edge onto the floor. Flames licked at her jeans leg.

Murdock patted the flames from Gabbie's clothes and pulled her to her feet. "Stay low. Less smoke." He raised his arm to cover his mouth and nose.

Gabbie pulled her shirt up over her face and turned, searching for the door.

Smoke and flames filled the room, making it impossible to see the way out.

Murdock squatted low and squinted into the swirling caldron of smoke and fire. For a long moment, he looked, slowly turning his head until he stopped and pointed. "There."

Gabbie looked below the rising smoke and spotted what he'd seen, the bottom half of a door.

Murdock slipped an arm around her and ducked low. "Let's go," he called out.

They'd taken one step when the ceiling above that door crashed to the floor, spewing flames and sparks.

"We have to go through that door. There's no other way," Murdock said.

"What are we waiting for?" Gabbie coughed up the smoke filling her lungs.

Murdock tucked her beneath his arm, shielding her body with his, and ran toward the burning ceiling boards between them and the door.

When they reached the pile of burning, smoking tinder, Murdock half-lifted, half-threw Gabbie over the flames and leaped after her.

Gabbie landed on the other side, fell to her knees, scrambled to her feet and lunged for the door. The heat and smoke bore down on her. If they didn't get out soon, they'd die.

She grabbed the door handle, yanked it open and dove out into the night air. Gabbie didn't stop until she was well away from the burning building that might once have been a house but would exist no more after that night.

With her focus on escaping a burning building, Gabbie didn't think about what lay beyond the walls of the old residence. Until she looked around and realized they were in the middle of the compound Lyssa had painstakingly drawn. Based on the frenzy of activity, the camp's occupants were packing up and bugging out in a helluva hurry.

Murdock grabbed Gabbie's hand and dragged her into the shadow of a metal shipping container. It provided just enough of a shadow to hide the two of them. From there, they could see most of what was happening in the light provided by several vehicles' headlights.

He touched his ear, expecting the radio earbud to be long gone. When it crackled with static, Murdock's eyes widened. "I can't believe it didn't fall out. The big question is, does it work?"

He tapped the earbud and spoke softly, "Nesting Eagle, this is Soaring Eagle back online."

"Soaring Eagle, this is Nesting Eagle. Glad you made it out," Drake's deep voice was hard to mistake. "Our flock is gathered, waiting.

"Soaring Eagle is in the Rat's Nest. Can you tell me what's happening?'"

"The Rat's Nest is moving. All the mice are

being loaded into old school buses. They'll leave as soon as the last child is on board."

"Fledgling?" Murdock asked.

Gabbie leaned in to hear the answer.

"Back with the others, taking charge and looking out for the littlest bird."

Gabbie pressed a hand to her chest and let out a sigh.

"Their Operation Bug-out can't leave," Murdock stressed.

"Working on it. Timing could be key. Backup is on its way. Operation Chicken Little ETA any minute."

"Moving closer to the buses," Murdock said. "Out here."

"How are we getting to the busses?" Gabbie asked.

"*We* don't. *I* do" He pointed to their position in the shadows. "You're going to stay here in the shadows and avoid being discovered."

"But there are two buses and only one of you," she argued. "What's your strategy?"

"Verify buses are being used to transport the children. If possible, hijack the bus and get it somewhere safe."

"Again, there's only one of you and two buses.

I've driven a bus before." Gabbie lifted her chin. "Besides, if you leave me here, you can't guarantee my safety."

Murdock's eyes narrowed. "Fine, but be quiet and stay in the shadows."

"Will do." Gabbie waited for Murdock to say the word.

Several men and young fighters dressed in black passed by carrying rifles.

Murdock and Gabbie shrank back against the storage container and waited until no one was around.

From where they stood, Gabbie could see that the number of boys and girls loading onto the buses had trickled to a few strays, some half-asleep, having been woken in the middle of the night.

The last girl out of what Gabbie assumed was the women's building had fiery red hair. She held the hand of a little girl, maybe three or four years old. "Lyssa and Samantha."

They climbed aboard the bus full of girls and made their way to the back.

"They're all loaded up," Gabbie said.

Murdock nodded. "It's time to roll."

CHAPTER 11

MURDOCK worried that Gabbie wasn't familiar with stealth warfare and would end up shot or captured.

If he had time, he'd hand off Gabbie to his teammates to be moved to a safe location. However, he couldn't wait. The buses were loaded. They'd be moving out soon if Murdock and Gabbie didn't do something quickly.

Without weapons, they had to rely on their brains. One thing going for them was the chaos of moving an entire camp. People were running around, trying to load everything into the trucks and trailers.

When they didn't have shadows to move into, Murdock and Gabbie kept their heads down and hurried along like anyone else working on getting everything out before morning.

"Hey, you!" a male voice called out beside Murdock. "Give me a hand."

Murdock turned to see a man dragging a crate out of a storage building. He started to turn away and keep going.

"Don't be an asshole," the man called out. "This box is heavy as fuck and can't be left behind."

Murdock had two choices. He could ignore the man and keep moving. The man would subsequently draw attention to him for being an asshole. Or Murdock could help the man and move on before he realized he didn't belong with TCW.

"Keep moving," he told Gabby. "I'll catch up."

Keeping her head down, Gabbie marched toward the corner of the next building, where she would wait in the shadows for Murdock to catch up.

With the buses in his peripheral vision and time ticking away, Murdock hurried over to help the man carry the crate to the back of a covered truck. As they tossed it up into the truck, the crate split open, and the contents spilled out onto the ground.

"Son of a bitch," the guy yelled and bent to retrieve a dozen AR-15 rifles. Murdock helped, tossing the weapons into the truck as fast as he could. All the while, he worried that Gabbie was alone and unprotected. That and the kids were loaded onto buses and could take off any minute. All the while, his gut was telling him he was running out of time.

He was tempted to snatch one of the rifles, but it would do him little good without ammunition.

As soon as the last rifle was loaded onto the truck, Murdock spun away. "Gotta go."

He ran to the building where he'd seen Gabbie stop and hide in the shadows.

She wasn't there.

Murdock moved to the next building and the next little bit of shadows she could have hidden in.

Still no Gabbie.

As he looked around the compound for the redhead, the bus full of girls moved forward, easing through the maze of trucks, trailers and people.

That's when he spotted Gabbie running alongside the bus.

A tractor-trailer rig blocked the main road through the compound, forcing the old school bus to stop while the truck driver worked to move to one side or the other of the gravel road to allow other traffic to move through.

With the bus stopped, Gabby quickly caught up.

Murdock, not so much. He was still half-walking and half-running, dodging people moving boxes and crates, almost tripping over boxes left on the ground.

Ahead, Gabby had reached the folding door and raised a fist to pound on it.

"Sweet Jesus, what is she doing?" he muttered beneath his breath and stretched into an all-out sprint.

The folding door opened, and a man carrying a gun dropped to the ground. As he turned toward Gabby, light from another truck's headlights shone on the man's face, revealing his trademark jagged scar.

The man aimed his rifle at Gabbie.

At that exact moment, armed men floated down from the sky, landing among the men and young people.

Shots were fired. People scattered.

Gabbie used the confusion to grab the barrel of Scarface's gun and shove it high. As she altered the weapon's aim, she kicked the man in the balls and pushed him until he fell backward, landing flat on his back on the hard ground, his rifle flying from his hands and landing a few feet away.

Murdock raced to Gabbie's assistance, but she was still too far away, and others moved into his path, slowing his progress.

With Scarface on the ground, Gabbie stepped around the man and bent to pick up the rifle, ejecting the magazine as her first order of business.

As she straightened, the man on the ground swept his leg out, knocking Gabbie off her feet. He rose behind her, grabbed his rifle and a handful of her hair and yanked her to an upright position.

"Let go of her," Murdock yelled. "Let her go, and I won't kill you."

Scarface snorted. "With what?"

"My bare hands are considered lethal weapons. Do you want to see if they've been rightly named?"

"Back off. There's one bullet left in the chamber. If you don't get the hell out of my face, I'll use it. On her." He pulled back hard on Gabbie's hair. Rage ripped through Murdock. If he had a weapon...

The man with the wicked scar held the rifle to

Gabbie's chin and backed toward the bus's open door, taking Gabbie inside with him.

The door closed behind him, and the bus moved forward and around the tractor-trailer rig.

"No," Murdock muttered. He ran to catch up, but the bus was moving faster than he could. As Hank's men settled to the ground, TCW men scattered. Trucks raced past Murdock. He tried to wave one down and almost got run over. The roar of a smaller engine drew his attention. A young man had just started the engine on his dirt bike and was fitting a helmet over his head, not ten yards from where Murdock stood.

Murdock raced toward him and arrived just as the man finished buckling the helmet beneath his chin. Before the guy knew what was happening, Murdock had yanked him off the back of his motorcycle. In one fluid motion, Murdock was on the bike, blasting past the trucks clogging the road in their exodus from the compound.

When he reached the highway, Murdock looked both ways, unsure which direction the bus would have gone. Other vehicles were going both ways—toward Last Resort or further west. Murdock turned toward Last Resort. He passed several trucks and vans, some pulling trailers, others bearing decals proclaiming them as members of The Chosen Way.

He'd begun to think he was going in the wrong direction when he spotted the bus ahead, going too fast for the curvy roads. Several times, the vehicle leaned hard on two wheels on a dangerous curve.

Not wanting to spur the driver to go faster, he slowed behind the bus and followed until the roads straightened, and they drove into Last Resort.

The bus driver blew through traffic lights and stop signs, barely slowing through the little town. On the other side of town, the bus picked up speed. Soon, they were blowing through Anaconda and heading for Butte.

With no way to board the bus and take out Scarface, the best Murdock could do was to follow until they arrived at their destination or ran out of gas. God forbid he ran out of gas first.

As soon as the man with the scarred face got Gabbie on the bus, he shoved her into the seat behind the driver and pointed the rifle at her. "Make one stupid move, and I'll use this rifle to put a bullet through your head." To the driver, he barked, "Drive, or I'll put the bullet through your head."

The driver shifted into gear and drove the bus through the compound past a tractor-trailer rig, several trucks being loaded and people on the ground, rushing around as if the world was coming to an end.

"What are you going to do with these girls?"

"None of your goddamn business," he snarled.

Gabbie didn't think she would get this man to turn the girls free just because she said he should, but she might buy time to figure out how to stop the bus and get the girls to safety. "Human trafficking is a federal crime punishable by imprisonment for anywhere from twenty years to life."

"Shut the fuck up," the man said.

She turned sideways in the seat and looked back at the frightened girls, huddled in their seats, holding on as the driver took the curves too fast. At one point, the bus was going so fast around a hairpin curve it leaned up on one side.

The girls screamed. Some slid out of their seats onto the floor.

"Shut up!" Scarface bellowed.

Near the back of the bus, Lyssa sat beside a child with white-blond hair and blue eyes. She couldn't be more than four years old. By the way Lyssa held her so close, reassuring and comforting her, the little girl had to be her little sister, Samantha. Lyssa had a bruise on her cheek. She'd probably gotten it as punishment for leaving the compound.

Gabbie's heart squeezed tightly in her chest. The girls were frightened and clinging to each other. They'd been through so much, and it wasn't over yet.

"So, how does Rayne Williams fit into what's going on at the compound?" Gabbie asked. "Is he selling girls into prostitution? Is that how he's amassed such a fortune?"

Scarface snorted. "He doesn't have to sell girls into the sex trade. What he does for them is give them skills, trains them well and they come out of the training with a career, the ability to earn their own money and a chance to see the world."

"Sounds too good to be true," Gabbie said. "And does all that justify him stealing them from their homes and traumatizing them for life?"

"Nobody wants these kids. They come from a broken foster care system or single-parent households where the parent works two jobs just to put a roof over their heads. He's doing them a favor."

The man nodded his head toward the girls on the bus. "He's doing all of them a favor. They won't be out stealing, doing drugs or getting drunk with their friends. They'll work and do as they're told."

"Against their will," Gabbie pointed out. "That's forced servitude and a federal crime."

Scarface held on as the bus careened around a corner. "Why do you care? They aren't your kids."

"They're children. They don't deserve what's happening to them. They should be allowed to have a childhood free of pain and suffering."

"Why should they? Not everyone has a happy childhood. You get what you get." He drew in a deep breath and blew it out. "You know, you just need to shut up. You hear me? Shut up."

Gabbie backed off, kept quiet and looked for opportunities to overtake the man with only one bullet in his gun. Once she disarmed him, he wouldn't be a threat anymore. She would get the driver to stop the bus, then she'd call Murdock and his friends, the state police and child protective services and get these children home. And she'd find a way to bring to justice Scarface, Rayne Williams and anyone else involved in abducting these children and forcing them into servitude.

She glanced out the window, keeping track of

where they were heading. They'd passed through Last Resort and Anaconda. They should be getting close to Butte soon. By now, the bus driver had broken every speed limit and had multiple counts of reckless driving. Surely, there was one law enforcement officer who wasn't on Rayne Williams' payroll.

Even if the police came after them, Gabbie wasn't sure the bus driver would pull over. He was as crazy as Scarface.

She couldn't just knock the two over the head. Not while they were speeding down a crooked highway with a busload of children.

If they slowed enough, she might have a chance. Or, if she could get control of the rifle with one bullet loaded in the chamber, would that be enough of a deterrent to scare the bus driver into pulling over?

She wished Murdock was there. They made a good team. He was adorable the way he swore he'd traded in his rifle for a nail gun and didn't want anything to do with protecting anyone. Yet, he'd sure volunteered to accompany her into a hot zone of crazies. If only he were with her now.

She glanced out the window and down the length of the bus to the rear window. She frowned.

The bus driver had passed other vehicles on straightaways and curves, leaving them all behind, except for the motorcycle that had been on their tail since Last Resort.

She squinted in an attempt to see who was on the motorcycle. The idiot was riding without a helmet. Didn't he know how dangerous that was?

And to follow a bus that close... Was that a traffic violation?

The rider had black hair and wore a black T-shirt. Gabbie had been wishing Murdock was with her so much her mind must be conjuring a look-alike.

Unless...

She half rose from her seat, staring out the back window. Was it...?

Gabbie sank down again. It was just wishful thinking.

Or was it?

Again, she rose from her seat.

This time Scarface poked her with the barrel of his rifle. "Sit!"

She did, hope swelling in her chest. Who would chase a bus on a motorcycle and follow it as far as they'd already come?

Someone who cared about the passengers

aboard the vehicle. Someone who might be able to help them. How? Gabbie didn't know. Just knowing he was following gave her that little bit of hope that helped her hold on and made her want to end this nightmare sooner rather than later, so she and Murdock could get back to getting to know each other.

He was an amazing man. After such a short time together, Gabbie was certain he was the man for her. But she was cautious by nature when it came to people. Giving them time was the prudent thing to do.

Then why was she ready to stop the bus, jump out and fling herself into his arms and declare her love for him?

Man, she had it bad. Once in the sack with the man and she was completely smitten.

Well, he was very good at what he did to her. She'd thought they'd have to try several times before achieving an orgasm. Her lips curled into a self-satisfied smile.

Murdock had taken her there in his first attempt. He'd shown her what it was like and how good it could be. Was it wrong of her to want more? If so, she could live with being wrong, as long as Murdock came with it.

As the bus driver approached Butte, he finally slowed to turn off the interstate at the exit for the Bert Mooney regional airport, located south of Butte.

Gabbie frowned. "Are we going to the airport?"

Scarface didn't respond.

Why would they be going to the airport with a busload of girls?

Then she recalled that Rayne Williams owned a plane and kept it at the Butte airport. He hadn't mentioned just how big that airplane was. They'd loaded the boys and the girls into buses. They had to be taking all of them to the same place.

Surely, he didn't plan on loading all the children into his plane and flying off to God knew where?

Her heart raced as the bus followed the signs to the airport. The good thing about going to the airport was that the bus driver had finally slowed to a reasonable speed. If she wanted to take the man's gun, now would be the perfect opportunity, especially since he wouldn't expect her to make an attempt after sitting so docilely for the past twenty minutes. Plus, Murdock was behind them as her backup.

The trouble was Scarface had one bullet in the

chamber. Gabbie couldn't risk that bullet hitting one of the children. She also couldn't risk getting shot by that bullet, leaving the children to Williams' nefarious plans. If he got them on that plane, he could take them out of the country. They'd never find their way back home, and their families would never have the resources to take the search abroad.

The bus driver slowed and turned onto the road leading to the general aviation terminal. As the bus turned, Gabbie pretended to slip off her seat, her body slamming into Scarface at the same time as she pushed the barrel of the rifle downward. If he pulled the trigger now, the bullet would go through the floor.

At least, that was the plan.

The execution was a little less graceful.

Yes, she slammed into Scarface and pointed the rifle's barrel at the floor.

That was where it deviated from her brilliant plan.

When she launched her attack, the bus driver got excited and swerved, throwing Gabbie and Scarface down the stairwell in a jumble of arms and legs with one rifle tangled between them.

It was a scramble for who was on top and who

had control of the rifle with one remaining bullet in the chamber.

Scarface ended up with the rifle in his hands, but as he tried to extricate himself from the tangle of arms and legs, he hit the trigger. The loud bang echoed inside the bus.

The girls screamed, and the bus driver swerved again, running over traffic cones and blowing through a chain link gate. They emerged on the tarmac, where the driver increased the speed of the bus as he raced toward a 727 with *RWSecurity* written in bold letters across the tail.

Gabbie rammed her elbow into Scarface's eye, stepped on his crotch with her heel and scrambled to her feet.

Lyssa had come to the front of the bus and stood beside the bus driver, her mouth set in a tight line.

Scarface struggled to his feet, still holding the rifle. "Bitch," snarled, "you'll pay for that."

As soon as he climbed two steps, Lyssa shoved the lever to open the folding doors.

Gabbie gave the man a crooked smile, cocked her leg and slammed her booted foot straight into the middle of his chest.

The man with the wicked scar on his face, still

holding the semi-automatic rifle, flew backward and out of the bus, landing hard on the tarmac.

The bus driver hunkered down and slammed his foot on the accelerator.

"Stop the bus," Gabbie demanded

When he didn't do as she said, Gabbie hooked her arm around the man's neck and squeezed as hard as she could.

His foot remained smashed to the accelerator as he headed straight for the 727.

"Stop the damned bus," Gabbie said through gritted teeth.

Lyssa dropped to her knees and pulled at the man's leg.

The driver went limp.

Lyssa pulled his foot off the accelerator and smashed the brake with both of her hands.

Gabbie reached over the driver's head, grabbed the steering wheel, and turned it away from the 727. Between the two of them, Gabbie and Lyssa brought the school bus to a halt without destroying an airplane or killing any of the children inside.

The motorcycle that had been following the bus from Last Resort pulled up to the open folding doors.

"Gabbie!" Murdock called out.

"I'm here," she said. "We're all right."

The 727's engines fired up, the roar deafening.

Gabbie pointed at the jet airplane. "That's Rayne William's plane," Gabbie yelled. "Don't let him get away."

Murdock twisted the throttle, sending the motorcycle flying across the tarmac.

The rear stairs to the plane started their slow closing sequence.

Gabbie held her breath as Murdock drove the motorcycle straight for the stairs.

Gabbie watched in horror as Murdock held his course all the way. At the last second, he turned the bike sideways and flung himself onto the retracting stairs. When he landed, the stairs were already halfway closed. The closing sequence continued until the stairs and Murdock disappeared inside.

The plane rolled away, taxiing to the end of the runway in preparation for takeoff.

"No, no, no." Gabbie whispered. If that plane took off, Murdock hadn't succeeded. In fact, they might have killed him. Then Rayne Williams would have gotten away with human trafficking and murder.

And Gabbie would go back to Eagle Rock alone. She wouldn't have had the opportunity to tell Murdock he was right. He was the one. She didn't need any more time to make sure. In her heart, she knew.

As the plane waited for the ATC to give them clearance to take off, tears slipped down Gabbie's cheeks. She's never been in love before. If she lost him now, how cruel was fate?

She swiped at the tears, squared her shoulders and focused on what her heart believed. He was all right. Murdock would be back.

The plane started down the runway. It had barely built up any speed when the engines geared back, and the aircraft slowed.

Two Montana State Police vehicles raced onto the runway and paced the 727 until it came to a complete halt.

The rear staircase made its slow descent.

Gabbie's pulse sped.

When the stairs touched the tarmac, Rayne Williams stepped down, dressed in a tailored charcoal suit, his head held high. The state police met him at the bottom of the stairs, cuffed him and led him to one of the service vehicles.

Behind him, wearing jeans, a T-shirt and work

boots, was the most handsome, courageous man Gabbie had fallen in love with. And he was heading her way.

She ran across the tarmac, straight into his arms. "I was so afraid."

He stroked her hair back from her face and bent to kiss her lips. "You were afraid for me?" He chuckled. "I was more afraid of that bus driver than jumping into that airplane."

"But you didn't know whether or not they were armed and ready to shoot." She shook her head. "I think I lost ten years of my life when that plane closed up tight. It was like it swallowed you. And when it taxied down to the end of the runway, I thought I'd never see you again."

Murdock tipped her chin up. "But I'm here now —all in one piece, with a bruise or two. And I'm ready to give you all the time in the world to get to know me and come to love me like I can't but love you. Baby, I'll wait until the end of time as long as there's even half a chance that you could love me."

She cupped his cheek in her hand. "There's not even half a chance of that."

Murdock frowned. "Really? Are you sure?"

She nodded. "There's no halfsies in this rela-tionship. I'm all in, one hundred percent in love with you." Gabbie laughed. "For someone who has always considered herself a bit of a control freak, I'm completely out of control with you and wouldn't have it any other way." She wrapped her arms around his neck, brought his mouth down to hers and kissed him like there would be no tomorrow.

Today, she'd been close to having no tomorrows with this man. She vowed that she would appreciate each and every day she was blessed to be in this man's life because he was the one, and they were meant to be.

EPILOGUE

Two weeks later...

"Hey, Murdock, how are the riding lessons going?" Drake asked from the other side of the long table full of the members of their construction team, their ladies, Molly McKinnon and her fiancé Parker, Hank Patterson and his computer guy, Swede.

"Good, actually. Little Joe hasn't run off with me in the four times I've ridden him. I count that as a win." Murdock grinned as he looked around at the men and women seated at the table and counted all his blessings. The number one blessing was seated to his right, Gabbie Myers.

He reached for her hand beneath the table and squeezed it gently.

"I thought it would be nice to bring you all together so you could hear what's taken place since the TCW compound was shut down." Hank turned to Swede. "You want to give them what you found and passed on to the FBI?"

Swede nodded. "Rayne Williams Security is a mercenary organization. Williams provides trained operatives to foreign dignitaries, wealthy clients and people with mafia connections who need an occasional cleanup job." Swede snorted. "Assassination."

"Wow," Gabbie said. "I had bad vibes about him from the moment we met. The horse I delivered had them, too."

"What happened to the stallion?" Hank asked.

Gabbie smiled. "The Double Diamond Ranch was able to refund the payment and reclaim the horse since Williams will be spending at least the next twenty years in jail for all his crimes. Hopefully, more. Anyway, the stallion is back on his home ranch, healthy and happy."

"That's good to know," Hank said. "Swede worked with the FBI to help them unravel the connection between Williams' mercenaries for hire and the people of The Chosen Way."

Swede nodded and continued, "Williams figured TCW would be a good front to confuse anyone inquiring about the children he was training to be soldiers and assassins. TCW wanted the combat and survival training necessary for post-apocalyptic scenarios. There was crossover, which helped disguise the fact he was brain-washing and training kids to fight battles in other countries."

Hank met Gabbie's gaze. "He'd just begun training girls because they make good surprise operatives, most countries wouldn't suspect. Apparently, there's big money in trained merce-nary soldiers if the training is proven. Williams' soldiers, younger and older, were highly qualified and extremely effective. He'd built up quite the reputation."

"It's one thing to hire adult mercenaries, but stealing children is just wrong," Murdock said.

Drake's fiancée, Cassie, leaned forward. "We have some more news that came out of a search of Rayne Williams' files. We found a name that could be good or bad." She took a deep breath and let it out. "One of the mercenaries on his database is

Penny Baker. Apparently, he didn't just abduct children. He took adults as well. The FBI is running the database against the missing persons database. They've already matched thirty names and think there are many more."

"That's amazing news." Dezi, Grimm's woman, said. "That gives us hope that Penny is alive. We just have to find her."

Murdock turned to Gabbie. "We have some news to share as well. Gabbie has agreed to be my wife."

Applause filled the dining room, and everyone wished them well.

"Thank you," Murdock said, happiness swelling his chest. "We're moving the wedding up to next weekend because we want to apply to adopt."

Gabbie's smile spread across her face. "We're going to adopt Lyssa and her little sister, Samantha."

Molly reached out and touched Gabbie's arm. "That's great news. They will be so lucky to have you as parents."

"We think we'll be the lucky ones to have Lyssa and Samantha as part of our family," Murdock said. It still felt strange to think he'd be going from confirmed bachelor to husband, father and family.

"And to think, none of this might've happened if not for a runaway horse." Gabbie laughed. "It was meant to be."

"You and I were meant to be. I can't imagine loving anyone more than I love you." He kissed her hand. "Remind me to give Little Joe an extra bucket of feed at my next lesson."

BREAKING SILENCE

DELTA FORCE STRONG BOOK #1

New York Times & *USA Today*
Bestselling Author

ELLE JAMES

BREAKING
Silence

DELTA FORCE STRONG

New York Times & USA Today Bestselling Author
ELLE JAMES

CHAPTER 1

HAD he known they would be deployed so soon after their last short mission to El Salvador, Rucker Sloan wouldn't have bought that dirt bike from his friend Duff. Now, it would sit there for months before he actually got to take it out to the track.

The team had been given forty-eight hours to pack their shit, take care of business and get onto the C130 that would transport them to Afghanistan.

Now, boots on the ground, duffel bags stowed in their assigned quarters behind the wire, they were ready to take on any mission the powers that be saw fit to assign.

What he wanted most that morning, after being

ELLE JAMES

awake for the past thirty-six hours, was a cup of strong, black coffee.

The rest of his team had hit the sack as soon as they got in. Rucker had already met with their commanding officer, gotten a brief introduction to the regional issues and had been told to get some rest. They'd be operational within the next forty-eight hours.

Too wound up to sleep, Rucker followed a stream of people he hoped were heading for the chow hall. He should be able to get coffee there.

On the way, he passed a sand volleyball court where two teams played against each other. One of the teams had four players, the other only three. The four-person squad slammed a ball to the ground on the other side of the net. The only female player ran after it as it rolled toward Rucker.

He stopped the ball with his foot and picked it up.

The woman was tall, slender, blond-haired and blue-eyed. She wore an Army PT uniform of shorts and an Army T-shirt with her hair secured back from her face in a ponytail seated on the crown of her head.

Without makeup, and sporting a sheen of

perspiration, she was sexy as hell, and the men on both teams knew it.

They groaned when Rucker handed her the ball. He'd robbed them of watching the female soldier bending over to retrieve the runaway.

She took the ball and frowned. "Do you play?"

"I have," he answered.

"We could use a fourth." She lifted her chin in challenge.

Tired from being awake for the past thirty-six hours, Rucker opened his mouth to say *hell no*. But he made the mistake of looking into her sky-blue eyes and instead said, "I'm in."

What the hell was he thinking?

Well, hadn't he been wound up from too many hours sitting in transit? What he needed was a little physical activity to relax his mind and muscles. At least, that's what he told himself in the split-second it took to step into the sandbox and serve up a heaping helping of whoop-ass.

He served six times before the team playing opposite finally returned one. In between each serve, his side gave him high-fives, all members except one—the blonde with the blue eyes he stood behind, admiring the length of her legs beneath her black Army PT shorts.

Twenty minutes later, Rucker's team won the match. The teams broke up and scattered to get showers or breakfast in the chow hall.

"Can I buy you a cup of coffee?" the pretty blonde asked.

"Only if you tell me your name." He twisted his lips into a wry grin. "I'd like to know who delivered those wicked spikes."

She held out her hand. "Nora Michaels," she said.

He gripped her hand in his, pleased to feel firm pressure. Women might be the weaker sex, but he didn't like a dead fish handshake from males or females. Firm and confident was what he preferred. Like her ass in those shorts.

She cocked an eyebrow. "And you are?"

He'd been so intent thinking about her legs and ass, he'd forgotten to introduce himself. "Rucker Sloan. Just got in less than an hour ago."

"Then you could probably use a tour guide to the nearest coffee."

He nodded. "Running on fumes here. Good coffee will help."

"I don't know about good, but it's coffee and it's fresh." She released his hand and fell in step beside him, heading in the direction of some of the others from their volleyball game.

"As long as it's strong and black, I'll be happy."

She laughed. "And awake for the next twenty-four hours."

"Spoken from experience?" he asked, casting a glance in her direction.

She nodded. "I work nights in the medical facility. It can be really boring and hard to stay awake when we don't have any patients to look after." She held up her hands. "Not that I want any of our boys injured and in need of our care."

"But it does get boring," he guessed.

"It makes for a long deployment." She held out her hand. "Nice to meet you, Rucker. Is Rucker a call sign or your real name?"

He grinned. "Real name. That was the only thing my father gave me before he cut out and left my mother and me to make it on our own."

"Your mother raised you, and you still joined the Army?" She raised an eyebrow. "Most mothers don't want their boys to go off to war."

"It was that or join a gang and end up dead in a gutter," he said. "She couldn't afford to send me to college. I was headed down the gang path when she gave me the ultimatum. Join and get the GI-Bill, or she would cut me off and I'd be out in the streets. To her, it was the only way to get me out of L.A. and to have the potential to go to college someday."

She smiled "And you stayed in the military."

He nodded. "I found a brotherhood that was better than any gang membership in LA. For now, I take college classes online. It was my mother's dream for me to graduate college. She never went, and she wanted so much more for me than the streets of L.A.. When my gig is up with the Army, if I haven't finished my degree, I'll go to college fulltime."

"And major in what?" Nora asked.

"Business management. I'm going to own my own security service. I want to put my combat skills to use helping people who need dedicated and specialized protection."

Nora nodded. "Sounds like a good plan."

"I know the protection side of things. I need to learn the business side and business law. Life will be different on the civilian side."

"True."

"How about you? What made you sign up?" he asked.

She shrugged. "I wanted to put my nursing

degree to good use and help our men and women in uniform. This is my first assignment after training."

"Drinking from the firehose?" Rucker stopped in front of the door to the mess hall.

She nodded. "Yes. But it's the best baptism under fire medical personnel can get. I'll be a better nurse for it when I return to the States."

"How much longer do you have to go?" he asked, hoping that she'd say she'd be there as long as he was. In his case, he never knew how long their deployments would last. One week, one month, six months...

She gave him a lopsided smile. "I ship out in a week."

"That's too bad." He opened the door for her. "I just got here. That doesn't give us much time to get to know each other."

"That's just as well." Nora stepped through the door. "I don't want to be accused of fraternizing. I'm too close to going back to spoil my record."

Rucker chuckled. "Playing volleyball and sharing a table while drinking coffee won't get you written up. I like the way you play. I'm curious to know where you learned to spike like that."

"I guess that's reasonable. Coffee first." She led him into the chow hall.

The smells of food and coffee made Rucker's mouth water.

He grabbed a tray and loaded his plate with eggs, toast and pancakes drenched in syrup. Last, he stopped at the coffee urn and filled his cup with freshly brewed black coffee.

When he looked around, he found Nora seated at one of the tables, holding a mug in her hands, a small plate with cottage cheese and peaches on it.

He strode over to her. "Mind if I join you?"

"As long as you don't hit on me," she said with cocked eyebrows.

"You say that as if you've been hit on before."

She nodded and sipped her steaming brew. "I lost count how many times in the first week I was here."

"Shows they have good taste in women and, unfortunately, limited manners."

"And you're better?" she asked, a smile twitching the corners of her lips.

"I'm not hitting on you. You can tell me to leave, and I'll be out of this chair so fast, you won't have time to enunciate the V."

She stared straight into his eyes, canted her head to one side and said, "Leave."

In the middle of cutting into one of his pancakes, Rucker dropped his knife and fork on the tray, shot out of his chair and left with his tray, sloshing coffee as he moved. He hoped she was just testing him. If she wasn't…oh, well. He was used to eating meals alone. If she was, she'd have to come to him.

He took a seat at the next table, his back to her, and resumed cutting into his pancake.

Nora didn't utter a word behind him.

Oh, well. He popped a bite of syrupy sweet pancake in his mouth and chewed thoughtfully. She was only there for another week. Man, she had a nice ass…and those legs… He sighed and bent over his plate to stab his fork into a sausage link.

"This chair taken?" a soft, female voice sounded in front of him.

He looked up to see the pretty blond nurse standing there with her tray in her hands, a crooked smile on her face.

He lifted his chin in silent acknowledgement.

She laid her tray on the table and settled onto the chair. "I didn't think you'd do it."

"Fair enough. You don't know me," he said.

"I know that you joined the Army to get out of street life. That your mother raised you after your father skipped out, that you're working toward a business degree and that your name is Rucker." She sipped her coffee.

He nodded, secretly pleased she'd remembered all that. Maybe there was hope for getting to know the pretty nurse before she redeployed to the States. And who knew? They might run into each other on the other side of the pond.

Still, he couldn't show too much interest, or he'd be no better than the other guys who'd hit on her. "Since you're redeploying back to the States in a week, and I'm due to go out on a mission, probably within the next twenty-four to forty-eight hours, I don't know if it's worth our time to get to know each other any more than we already have."

She nodded. "I guess that's why I want to sit with you. You're not a danger to my perfect record of no fraternizing. I don't have to worry that you'll fall in love with me in such a short amount of time." She winked.

He chuckled. "As I'm sure half of this base has fallen in love with you since you've been here."

She shrugged. "I don't know if it's love, but it's damned annoying."

"How so?"

She rolled her eyes toward the ceiling. "I get flowers left on my door every day."

"And that's annoying? I'm sure it's not easy coming up with flowers out here in the desert." He set down his fork and took up his coffee mug. "I think it's sweet." He held back a smile. Well, almost.

"They're hand-drawn on notepad paper and left on the door of my quarters and on the door to the shower tent." She shook her head. "It's kind of creepy and stalkerish."

Rucker nodded. "I see your point. The guys should at least have tried their hands at origami flowers, since the real things are scarce around here."

Nora smiled. "I'm not worried about the pictures, but the line for sick call is ridiculous."

"How so?"

"So many of the guys come up with the lamest excuses to come in and hit on me. I asked to work the nightshift to avoid sick call altogether."

"You have a fan group." He smiled. "Has the adoration gone to your head?"

She snorted softly. "No."

"You didn't get this kind of reaction back in the States?"

"I haven't been on active duty for long. I only decided to join the Army after my mother passed away. I was her fulltime nurse for a couple years as she went through stage four breast cancer. We thought she might make it." Her shoulders sagged. "But she didn't."

"I'm sorry to hear that. My mother meant a lot to me, as well. I sent money home every month after I enlisted and kept sending it up until the day she died suddenly of an aneurysm."

"I'm so sorry about your mother's passing," Nora said, shaking her head. "Wow. As an enlisted man, how did you make enough to send some home?"

"I ate in the chow hall and lived on post. I didn't party or spend money on civilian clothes or booze. Mom needed it. I gave it to her."

"You were a good son to her," Nora said.

His chest tightened. "She died of an aneurysm a couple of weeks before she was due to move to Texas where I'd purchased a house for her."

"Wow. And, let me guess, you blame yourself for not getting her to Texas sooner...?" Her gaze captured his.

Her words hit home, and he winced. "Yeah. I should've done it sooner."

"Can't bring people back with regrets." Nora stared into her coffee cup. "I learned that. The only thing I could do was move forward and get on with living. I wanted to get away from Milwaukee and the home I'd shared with my mother. Not knowing where else to go, I wandered past a realtor's office and stepped into a recruiter's office. I had my nursing degree, they wanted and needed nurses on active duty. I signed up, they put me through some officer training and here I am." She held her arms out.

"Playing volleyball in Afghanistan, working on your tan during the day and helping soldiers at night." Rucker gave her a brief smile. "I, for one, appreciate what you're doing for our guys and gals."

"I do the best I can," she said softly. "I just wish I could do more. I'd rather stay here than redeploy back to the States, but they're afraid if they keep us here too long, we'll burn out or get PTSD."

"One week, huh?"

She nodded. "One week."

"In my field, one week to redeploy back to the

States is a dangerous time. Anything can happen and usually does."

"Yeah, but you guys are on the frontlines, if not behind enemy lines. I'm back here. What could happen?"

Rucker flinched. "Oh, sweetheart, you didn't just say that..." He glanced around, hoping no one heard her tempt fate with those dreaded words *What could happen?*

Nora grinned. "You're not superstitious, are you?"

"In what we do, we can't afford not to be," he said, tossing salt over his shoulder.

"I'll be fine," she said in a reassuring, nurse's voice.

"Stop," he said, holding up his hand. "You're only digging the hole deeper." He tossed more salt over his other shoulder.

Nora laughed.

"Don't laugh." He handed her the saltshaker. "Do it."

"I'm not tossing salt over my shoulder. Someone has to clean the mess hall."

Rucker leaned close and shook salt over her shoulder. "I don't know if it counts if someone else throws salt over your shoulder, but I figure you now need every bit of luck you can get."

"You're a fighter but afraid of a little bad luck." Nora shook her head. "Those two things don't seem to go together."

"You'd be surprised how easily my guys are freaked by the littlest things."

"And you," she reminded him.

"You asking *what could happen?* isn't a little thing. That's in-your-face tempting fate." Rucker was laying it on thick to keep her grinning, but deep down, he believed what he was saying. And it didn't make a difference the amount of education he had or the statistics that predicted outcomes. His gut told him she'd just tempted fate with her statement. Maybe he was overthinking things. Now, he was worried she wouldn't make it back to the States alive.

NORA LIKED RUCKER. He was the first guy who'd walked away without an argument since she'd arrived at the base in Afghanistan. He'd meant what he'd said and proved it. His dark brown hair and deep green eyes, coupled with broad shoulders and a narrow waist, made him even more attractive. Not all the men were in as good a shape as Rucker. And he seemed to have a very determined attitude.

She hadn't known what to expect when she'd deployed. Being the center of attention of almost every single male on the base hadn't been one of her expectations. She'd only ever considered herself average in the looks department. But when the men outnumbered women by more than ten to one, she guessed average appearance moved up in the ranks.

"Where did you learn to play volleyball?" Rucker asked, changing the subject of her leaving and her flippant comment about what could happen in one week.

"I was on the volleyball team in high school. It got me a scholarship to a small university in my home state of Minnesota, where I got my Bachelor of Science degree in Nursing."

"It takes someone special to be a nurse," he stated. "Is that what you always wanted to be?"

She shook her head. "I wanted to be a firefighter when I was in high school."

"What made you change your mind?"

She stared down at the coffee growing cold in

her mug. "My mother was diagnosed with cancer when I was a senior in high school. I wanted to help but felt like I didn't know enough to be of assistance." She looked up. "She made it through chemo and radiation treatments and still came to all of my volleyball games. I thought she was in the clear."

"She wasn't?" Rucker asked, his tone low and gentle.

"She didn't tell me any different. When I got the scholarship, I told her I wanted to stay close to home to be with her. She insisted I go and play volleyball for the university. I was pretty good and played for the first two years I was there. I quit the team in my third year to start the nursing program. I didn't know there was anything wrong back home. I called every week to talk to Mom. She never let on that she was sick." She forced a smile. "But you don't want my sob story. You probably want to know what's going on around here."

He set his mug on the table. "If we were alone in a coffee bar back in the States, I'd reach across the table and take your hand."

"Oh, please. Don't do that." She looked around the mess hall, half expecting someone might have overheard Rucker's comment. "You're enlisted. I'm an officer. That would get us into a whole lot of trouble."

"Yeah, but we're also two human beings. I wouldn't be human if I didn't feel empathy for you and want to provide comfort."

She set her coffee cup on the table and laid her hands in her lap. "I'll be satisfied with the thought. Thank you."

"Doesn't seem like enough. When did you find out your mother was sick?"

She swallowed the sadness that welled in her throat every time she remembered coming home to find out her mother had been keeping her illness from her. "It wasn't until I went home for Christmas in my senior year that I realized she'd been lying to me for a while." She laughed in lieu of sobbing. "I don't care who they are, old people don't always tell the truth."

"How long had she been keeping her sickness from you?"

"She'd known the cancer had returned halfway through my junior year. I hadn't gone home that summer because I'd been working hard to get my coursework and clinical hours in the nursing program. When I went home at Christmas..." Nora gulped. "She wasn't the same person. She'd lost so much weight and looked twenty years older."

"Did you stay home that last semester?" Rucker asked.

"Mom insisted I go back to school and finish what I'd started. Like your mother, she hadn't gone to college. She wanted her only child to graduate. She was afraid that if I stayed home to take care of her, I wouldn't finish my nursing degree."

"I heard from a buddy of mine that those programs can be hard to get into," he said. "I can see why she wouldn't want you to drop everything in your life to take care of her."

Nora gave him a watery smile. "That's what she said. As soon as my last final was over, I returned to my hometown. I became her nurse. She lasted another three months before she slipped away."

"That's when you joined the Army?"

She shook her head. "Dad was so heartbroken, I stayed a few months until he was feeling better. I got a job at a local emergency room. On weekends, my father and I worked on cleaning out the house and getting it ready to put on the market."

"Is your dad still alive?" Rucker asked.

Nora nodded. "He lives in Texas. He moved to a small house with a big backyard." She forced a smile.

"He has a garden, and all the ladies in his retirement community think he's the cat's meow. He still misses Mom, but he's getting on with his life."

Rucker tilted his head. "When did you join the military?"

"When Dad sold the house and moved into his retirement community. I worried about him, but he's doing better."

"And you?"

"I miss her. But she'd whip my ass if I wallowed in self-pity for more than a moment. She was a strong woman and expected me to be the same."

Rucker grinned. "From what I've seen, you are."

Nora gave him a skeptical look. "You've only seen me playing volleyball. It's just a game." Not that she'd admit it, but she was a real softy when it came to caring for the sick and injured.

"If you're half as good at nursing, which I'm willing to bet you are, you're amazing." He started to reach across the table for her hand. Before he actually touched her, he grabbed the saltshaker and shook it over his cold breakfast.

"You just got in this morning?" Nora asked.

Rucker nodded.

"How long will you be here?" she asked.

"I don't know."

"What do you mean, you don't know? I thought when people were deployed, they were given a specific timeframe."

"Most people are. We're deployed where and when needed."

Nora frowned. "What are you? Some kind of special forces team?"

His lips pressed together. "Can't say."

She sat back. He was some kind of Special Forces. "Army, right?"

He nodded.

That would make him Delta Force. The elite of the elite. A very skilled soldier who undertook incredibly dangerous missions. She gulped and stopped herself from reaching across the table to take his hand. "Well, I hope all goes well while you and your team are here."

"Thanks."

A man hurried across the chow hall wearing shorts and an Army T-shirt. He headed directly toward their table.

Nora didn't recognize him. "Expecting some-one?" she asked Rucker, tipping her head toward the man.

Rucker turned, a frown pulling his eyebrows together. "Why the hell's Dash awake?"

Nora frowned. "Dash? Please tell me that's his callsign, not his real name."

Rucker laughed. "It should be his real name. He's first into the fight, and he's fast." Rucker stood and faced his teammate. "What's up?"

"CO wants us all in the Tactical Operations Center," Dash said. "On the double."

"Guess that's my cue to exit." Rucker turned to Nora. "I enjoyed our talk."

She nodded. "Me, too."

Dash grinned. "Tell you what...I'll stay and finish your conversation while you see what the commander wants."

Rucker hooked Dash's arm twisted it up behind his back, and gave him a shove toward the door. "You heard the CO, he wants all of us." Rucker winked at Nora. "I hope to see you on the volleyball court before you leave."

"Same. Good luck." Nora's gaze followed Rucker's broad shoulders and tight ass out of the chow hall. Too bad she'd only be there another week before she shipped out. She would've enjoyed more volleyball and coffee with the Delta Force operative.

He'd probably be on maneuvers that entire week.

She stacked her tray and coffee cup in the collection area and left the chow hall, heading for the building where she shared her quarters with Beth Drennan, a nurse she'd become friends with during their deployment together.

As close as they were, Nora didn't bring up her conversation with the Delta. With only a week left at the base, she probably wouldn't run into him again. Though she would like to see him again, she prayed he didn't end up in the hospital.

Breaking Silence (#1)

ABOUT THE AUTHOR

ELLE JAMES also writing as MYLA JACKSON is a *New York Times* and *USA Today* Bestselling author of books including cowboys, intrigues and paranormal adventures that keep her readers on the edges of their seats. When she's not at her computer, she's traveling, snow skiing, boating, or riding her ATV, dreaming up new stories. Learn more about Elle James at www.ellejames.com

Website | Facebook | Twitter | GoodReads | Newsletter | BookBub | Amazon

Or visit her alter ego Myla Jackson at mylajackson.com
Website | Facebook | Twitter | Newsletter

Follow Me!
www.ellejames.com
ellejamesauthor@gmail.com

ALSO BY ELLE JAMES

Shadow Assassin

Delta Force Strong

Brotherhood Protectors Yellowstone

Saving Savvie (#6)

Iron Horse Legacy

Playing With Fire (#5)

Up in Flames (#6)

Total Meltdown (#7)

Declan's Defenders

Marine Force Recon (#1)

Show of Force (#2)

Full Force (#3)

Driving Force (#4)

Tactical Force (#5)

Disruptive Force (#6)

Mission: Six

One Intrepid SEAL

Two Dauntless Hearts

Three Courageous Words

Four Relentless Days

Five Ways to Surrender

Six Minutes to Midnight

Hearts & Heroes Series

Wyatt's War (#1)

Mack's Witness (#2)

Ronin's Return (#3)

Sam's Surrender (#4)

Take No Prisoners Series

SEAL's Honor (#1)

SEAL'S Desire (#2)

SEAL's Embrace (#3)

SEAL's Obsession (#4)

SEAL's Proposal (#5)

SEAL's Seduction (#6)

SEAL'S Defiance (#7)

SEAL's Deception (#8)

SEAL's Deliverance (#9)

SEAL's Ultimate Challenge (#10)

Texas Billionaire Club

Tarzan & Janine (#1)

Something To Talk About (#2)

Who's Your Daddy (#3)

Love & War (#4)

Billionaire Online Dating Service

The Billionaire Husband Test (#1)

The Billionaire Cinderella Test (#2)

The Billionaire Bride Test (#3)

The Billionaire Daddy Test (#4)

The Billionaire Matchmaker Test (#5)

The Billionaire Glitch Date (#6)

The Billionaire Perfect Date (#7) coming soon

The Billionaire Replacement Date (#8) coming soon

The Billionaire Wedding Date (#9) coming soon

Ballistic Cowboy

Hot Combat (#1)

Hot Target (#2)

Hot Zone (#3)

Hot Velocity (#4)

Cajun Magic Mystery Series

Voodoo on the Bayou (#1)

Voodoo for Two (#2)

Deja Voodoo (#3)

Cajun Magic Mysteries Books 1-3

SEAL Of My Own

Navy SEAL Survival

Navy SEAL Captive

Navy SEAL To Die For

Navy SEAL Six Pack

Devil's Shroud Series

Deadly Reckoning (#1)

Deadly Engagement (#2)

Deadly Liaisons (#3)

Deadly Allure (#4)

Deadly Obsession (#5)

Deadly Fall (#6)

Covert Cowboys Inc Series

Triggered (#1)

Taking Aim (#2)

Bodyguard Under Fire (#3)

Cowboy Resurrected (#4)

Navy SEAL Justice (#5)

Navy SEAL Newlywed (#6)

High Country Hideout (#7)

Clandestine Christmas (#8)

Thunder Horse Series

Hostage to Thunder Horse (#1)

Thunder Horse Heritage (#2)

Thunder Horse Redemption (#3)

Christmas at Thunder Horse Ranch (#4)

Demon Series

Hot Demon Nights (#1)

Demon's Embrace (#2)

Tempting the Demon (#3)

Lords of the Underworld

Witch's Initiation (#1)

Witch's Seduction (#2)

The Witch's Desire (#3)

Possessing the Witch (#4)

Stealth Operations Specialists (SOS)

Nick of Time

Alaskan Fantasy

Boys Behaving Badly Anthologies

Rogues (#1)

Blue Collar (#2)

Pirates (#3)

Made in the USA
Middletown, DE
11 January 2023

21804900R00150